ONCE UPON A TIME, BEN MOON WAS THE DEADLIEST GUNMAN IN THE WEST

Ben Moon awoke to the sound of the ice breaking in the river. It sounded like the breaking of bones. He awoke cold and shivering even though he had two blankets covering him. The damned whiskey! Kept his blood all thinned out. Winters came hard in Montana Territory. No place for a man who likes his whiskey and lives in a Chinaman's shack with cracks between the boards so wide you can stick a finger through.

He rolled onto his side, drew his knees up, and tried hard to ignore the cold futile air of the shack. He lay there a long time, awake, gritting his teeth against the cold, listening to the ice break in the river.

His union suit was damp cold from the whiskey sweats. The whiskey and the dreams. He reached a hand out for the bottle, knocked it over; it rang empty.

"Damn," he muttered. Bringing his hand up to his face, he felt the raspy stubble of old beard. Tracing his fingers along the line of his jaw, he touched the smoothness of the scar there, reached upwards above the brow, felt another, smaller scar there.

Slowly, he sat up on the side of the bed, making sure to keep one of the blankets draped over his shoulders as he did so. The ice breaking up in the river was a sure sign of spring, but the coldness of the room lent no promise of warm days ahead.

He sure wished he had some more whiskey.

HE'D FALLEN A LONG WAY.

BILL BROOKS
MOON'S BLOOD

ZEBRA BOOKS
KENSINGTON PUBLISHING CORP.

ZEBRA BOOKS are published by

Kensington Publishing Corp.
850 Third Avenue
New York, NY 10022

First Printing: July, 1994

Printed in the United States of America

For Diane, who taught me about love and living the dream.

Prologue

The man standing at the long bar in the Miss Lilly Saloon wore a linen duster, a sweat-stained Stetson with a curled brim, and a look of weariness. He sipped whiskey and stood alone.

Outside, the wind whistled along the boardwalk carrying with it dust and tumbleweeds and hope.

There was something else outside: The body of a man tied belly-down over the back of a steeldust mare. The man's coal-black hair fluttered in the wind.

Tied up next to the steeldust was a big, blood-bay gelding. Both animals were damp with sweat.

The man sipped the whiskey slowly, felt its bite, and stood it. Another hundred miles to go, he thought to himself. He knew already that there were folks gathered around outside staring and whispering about the curiosity he had dragged into their town. A dead man was a greater curiosity than a circus or an opera singer.

Every town he had ridden through, they had come out to see the body of Claude Highsmith: Desperado, shootist, killer, and now dead man.

A photographer over in Montgomery Creek had offered to pay three dollars to take the dead man's photograph, and a woman in Bayless had tried to snip a lock of hair from the corpse.

A bartender in Waylo had offered fifty dollars for Claude Highsmith's trigger finger. He'd wanted to put it in a jar of brine and charge a dime a person to have a look at it.

A hundred more miles, he thought and drained the whiskey glass.

Commotion in the doorway drew his attention. The man in the linen duster looked up, saw first his reflection in the mirror behind the bar, then saw several men crowding through the double doors behind him.

"That's him," said someone in the group.

He felt nerves that were already raw from the journey twang like old piano wires inside him. He turned to face the men. As he did so, the linen duster parted, revealing the double-action .44 Starr revolver he wore. Revealed, also, was the small silver badge pinned to his inner coat.

The faces didn't mean much. Ranchers, clerks, lawyers, and pious preachers. One face, though, held his attention: A straw-haired youth with bad skin standing to the fore of the others. It was easy to see the kid had been drinking.

The kid had a nickel-plated Colt Peacemaker with gutta-percha grips sticking from his belt.

"You Ben Moon?" The kid's voice was thin and high—womanly. When the man in the linen duster failed to answer, the kid made his first mistake: He took the silence to mean weakness.

"You the one that killed Claude Highsmith?"

He didn't feel it necessary to engage in idle conversation, especially with a kid made tough on whiskey; he had neither the time nor the desire. Dallas was still a hundred miles away and it wasn't getting any closer.

"Move away, boy."

The kid stiffened, those backing him drifted away.

"You tell me first whether you're Ben Moon or not!"

It wasn't worth killing somebody over a question, even if it were a question he didn't care to answer.

"I am."

"You personally kill Claude Highsmith?"

"I did."

"Did you shoot him in the back, mister? I can't see you taking Claude Highsmith unless you shot him in the back, not even you."

"You're pushing your luck, boy!"

The florid-faced bartender came around the end of the bar and said, "Charley, get your young ass out of here! Go on home!"

The kid's eyes narrowed. The bad complexion flushed pink.

"You go to hell, Joe Barber!"

Suddenly the Colt was in the kid's hand, the seven-and-a-half-inch barrel wavering between the bartender and the man in the linen duster.

It had come to this, he thought: Getting killed by a damn wet-nose kid. Son of a bitch!

"Now what do you think, Mr. Ben Moon? What'll folks think when they see I killed the man who killed Claude Highsmith? Reckon they'll take notice?"

"I reckon they will, kid."

"Yeah, goddamnit! I reckon they will, too!"

It wasn't true, he thought as he stood there staring down the barrel of the cocked Colt—his whole life was not passing through his mind as he'd heard tell it did when a man was about to die. Hell, not even one friend showed up to say goodbye.

He just hoped the kid's aim would be true, find its mark,

and leave him stone-cold dead. He had been shot before, and it had hurt like hell. He didn't want to *just* get shot again.

But, the way the kid was waving the pistol around, it wasn't likely it was going to be a clean shot.

The kid had a tic just under his left eye. Sweat glistened on his cheeks. He'd mess his pants; they always did.

The movement was old and familiar and swift. But not so swift as to prevent the kid from pulling the trigger on the Colt.

The hammer fell with a click.

The Starr banged hard and spewed a cloud of gray smoke.

The slug caught the kid dead center, just above the belt buckle, and flung him onto his back; the Colt clattered across the floor.

For a long moment, there was a silence in the room so immense that it seemed as though time itself had simply stopped.

The kid groaned softly; his head rolled from left to right. He could smell the beer-soaked sawdust. He thought he could smell something burning.

The bartender knelt by the boy, took his wrist, and looked into the confused eyes.

"You've been gutshot, Charley."

"Have I?" he asked, gritting his teeth and raising his head to study the spreading stain on his shirtfront.

"I can't feel my legs," he said softly.

The bartender shook his head.

"I thought I . . ."

Tears leaked out of the corner of the kid's eyes.

"Tell Mama. . . . Tell her I got shot."

"Somebody get a doctor," the bartender said. Then, it

was decided that it would be better just to pick the kid up and carry him to the doctor's office. He cried out when they lifted him. Blood leaked from him and splattered the floor and the boots of the men that carried him.

The bartender wiped his hands on the apron tied around his waist.

"He'll die."

Ben Moon acknowledged the fact with a nod. He knocked the spent shell from his pistol and replaced it with a fresh load.

"Gutshot is a terrible way to die," said the bartender.

The man in the linen duster placed both hands on top of the bar and seemed to stare at them for a long time.

"I reckon so," he said.

"You maybe didn't have to shoot him in the guts, mister."

"Are you still selling your whiskey?" asked Ben Moon. The bartender nodded.

"Then pour."

There was a long time of silence; everything seemed to take on a slowness about it.

The afternoon light slanted in through the doorway and touched the back wall where an upright piano stood silent and unused. A Regulator clock ticked on the wall, its brass pendulum catching pieces of the light.

"You didn't have to shoot that boy in the guts," repeated the bartender.

The man in the linen duster swallowed the whiskey in the glass and deliberately stood the empty glass upside down on the bar. *How could he explain it—that he hadn't meant to gutshoot the kid; that it was his own fear, and lost skills, that had gutshot the kid.*

His clear, colorless gaze came to rest on the florid face of the bartender.

After a hard moment of staring, he turned slowly away from the bar, noticed that there were others staring at him, standing in the shadows and recesses.

The doorway was framed in brassy light. He walked toward it. His spurs rang with each step. It sounded like the tolling of small bells.

From somewhere in the shadows he heard his name being whispered: *Ben Moon.* It sounded like someone speaking the end of a prayer, like: *Amen.*

He mounted the blood bay, took the lead rope of the steeldust that carried the dead man upon its back, and then followed the west road.

A hundred more miles he thought to himself.

One

Ben Moon awoke to the sound of the ice breaking in the river. It sounded like the breaking of bones. He awoke cold and shivering even though he had two blankets covering him. The damn whiskey! Kept his blood all thinned out. Winters came hard in Montana Territory. No place for a man who likes his whiskey and lives in a Chinaman's shack with cracks between the boards so wide you can stick a finger through.

He rolled unto his side, drew his knees up, and tried hard to ignore the cold futile air of the shack.

He lay there for a time, awake, gritting his teeth against the cold, listening to the ice break on the river.

Two blankets ain't enough, he told himself. Next year, I'm getting three. It was a small promise to himself, but a promise nonetheless.

His union suit was damp cold from the sweats the whiskey had given him. The whiskey and the dreams. Not dreams really, but nightmares. He reached a hand out for the bottle, knocked it over; it rang empty.

"Damn," he muttered. Bringing his hand up to his face, he felt the raspy stubble of old beard. Tracing his fingers along the line of his jaw, he touched the smoothness of the scar there, reached upwards above the brow, felt another, smaller scar there.

Slowly, he sat up on the side of the bed, making sure to keep one of the blankets draped over his shoulders as he did so.

The ice breaking in the river was a sure sign of spring, but the coldness of the room lent no promise of warm days ahead.

His gaze went to one of two small windows in the cabin. The panes of glass were grimy and smudged with coal-oil soot, but a fair amount of pearl light still shone through, enough so that he had to squint to keep it from hurting his eyes.

He was wont not to let his bare feet touch the earthen floor, but the urge to make water made it impossible to simply sit there and not get up.

Surprisingly, the air outside seemed warmer than that in the cabin. He walked out back away from the cabin to answer nature's call and promptly returned.

The sun stood up tall and too bright to look directly at the cornflower-blue sky that touched the mountains all around the valley and glinted off their snow-covered peaks.

Ben Moon's breath came out in faint frosty puffs and he blew into his hands and stamped his feet against the cold ground.

He picked up a few chunks of wood from a dwindling pile outside the cabin's door and shoved them into the small stove that stood in the center of the cabin.

Fumbling with a box of matches and a page of newspaper that was dated June 15, 1881—printed ten months previously—he was able to raise a fire. A half-pot of yesterday's coffee sat atop the burner plate. All it needed was heating up.

He waited until he saw little chuffs of steam coming from

the spout of the coffeepot before pouring a tin cupful and sitting back down on the edge of the bed.

Slowly, he sipped the black, bitter liquid. It was worse than bile.

He sat there feeling caught up in himself, caught up in his times, caught up in the emptiness of the land and the emptiness of his life.

He sure wished he had some more whiskey.

He sat listening to the ice break in the river and sipped his bilious coffee and felt old aches and pains haunt his body as much as old memories haunted his mind.

Nights were terribly bad because of the nightmares; days didn't seem much better because of the empty sameness.

He heard the cry of a red-tail hawk as it soared somewhere outside scouting for a meal. He had almost shot that hawk last winter when he had gotten so damn hungry for something besides jerky and corn dodgers.

He had taken his Henry outside and sat on a rock and watched the red tail for nearly an hour as it circled over the river and along the woods on either side.

That old hawk had seen him, too, and maintained its distance. But still, he could have shot it clean to pieces if he had wanted to. He could still shoot, by God!

But there had been something both painful and magnificent in the cry of that old bird. Something that had said: Don't shoot me, mister; I'm just looking for a meal same as you. So he hadn't shot. He'd caught a turtle down by the river instead and boiled it up and had a fine turtle stew. And the day after, three or four jackrabbits the size of working dogs had come up and presented themselves to him and he had shot two of them and had rabbit stew that night and the next couple of days as well.

He had thrown out the guts for the hawk.

He heard something off in the distance. Waited, sipped the coffee. The something drew nearer.

It proved to be the rattle of a spring wagon.

He went to the door, stood at the threshold—the blanket draped over his shoulders, the tin coffee cup held in both hands.

A large, dark-skinned man wearing his hair braided drove the wagon. He pulled back on the reins of the big, bony gray horse that was pulling the wagon and brought it to a jarring halt.

Ben Moon wasn't quite sure whether the unexpected visit of Ned Bluecorn was a welcome sight or not. They had known each other for a time, but he had always figured there was something about the Blackfoot that no white man could fully trust. The old bastard had eyes like a buzzard and no doubt still carried old grudges.

"I see you are still alive," said the Indian.

"I ain't so damn sure," said Ben Moon. "It doesn't feel like it."

A slow smile spread across the broad dark face of the Blackfoot.

"I keep thinking maybe someday I'll come out here and find you dead."

"You mean you keep hoping," said Moon.

"Well, maybe that, too. I could use a nice cabin like this one you got yourself here." The comment was derisive; the look the Blackfoot tossed in with it was one of dark-eyed condemnation of the white man's living quarters.

"It beats sleeping on the ground," said Ben Moon, without taking exception to the Blackfoot's remarks.

"Could use me that Henry rifle of yours and that Starr pistol with them fancy grips you keep hidden under your pillow."

"I suppose you could use my horse and saddle, too."

"That old gelding of yours don't seem worth much," said Ned Bluecorn casting his buzzard eyes toward the lone blood-bay horse in the corral. "But I could maybe get fifty dollars for him in town if I was to sell him to an emigrant and throw in your saddle, too."

"Well, as you can see, I'm still alive somewhat, so I guess you've wasted your time driving all the way out here."

"Naw, Jane sent me to deliver you some groceries. Said you'd most likely be starved to death by now." The man in the wagon eyed the leanness of the man in the doorway, figured he had seen corpses over at Stolly's Funeral Parlor that looked in better condition.

"Well, you might as well climb down then; my feet are getting cold standing out here."

Ben Moon watched the large Blackfoot lower his bulk from the wagon, saw how the wagon sat up a few inches higher after he did so.

Ned Bluecorn spat a stream of whiskey-colored tobacco juice into a dwindling patch of snow, then grabbed a gunny sack from the back of the wagon and headed for the cabin.

He was as bowlegged as a cowboy.

Ben Moon sliced off some of the bacon the Blackfoot had brought him and threw it into a large, black iron pan. He tossed out the old grounds from the coffeepot and put in some fresh ones, pinching out a dead beetle as he did so.

Neither man said anything while the meal was being prepared.

Later, after they'd eaten, they moved out to the fragmented porch of the cabin and smoked cigarettes.

"You ought to do something with this place," said Ned Bluecorn looking up at the patches of sky that could be seen in the overhang where the wind had blown the shingles off.

"What do you suggest?"

"Burn it down, maybe."

"A man wouldn't have much if he went around burning down everything that just needed a little fixing. Besides, it's sort of like home."

Ned Bluecorn squatted on his heels, his forearms resting upon his knees, his dark mysterious gaze staring out to an open expanse of land that led to the river.

"The ice is bustin' up in the river," he said.

"I know. It woke me up," said Ben Moon, trying to roll another shuck with unsteady fingers.

"How's Jane?"

"She's been sick—coughing mostly."

"It's the damn winters out here. They're enough to kill anybody."

"Why do you stay then?"

He finally got the cigarette rolled and put to his lips.

"Hell, I don't know why I came here and why I've stayed here other than it's sort of to hell and gone from anyplace else."

The Blackfoot turned his head slowly to look at the man who sat in the cane-bottomed chair, his blanket draped over his shoulders and a lit cigarette dangling from his lips.

"You sure don't look like no famous gunfighter to me."

"I ain't."

"You was once, or so it's said."

"I used to be a lot of things that I'm not anymore."

"Jane says she'd like to see you soon as you could come."

"How sick is she, Ned?"

"Pretty sick."

"Is she dying?"

"Yeah. I think maybe she is."

From the corner of his eye, Ned Bluecorn saw the tired-looking white man's reddened eyes look over at him; saw, too, the bob of Adam's apple beneath the grizzled, weathered skin.

It was hard news. Whether you said it or whether you heard it. Ned Bluecorn knew that Ben Moon wasn't going to comment on it further than the look, the hard swallow.

"I tried to get her to marry me. She said no. I asked was it because I was an Indian. You know what she said to me?"

"What?"

"Said she'd marry me in a minute except I'd make her haul wood and carry water and do it like dogs do it and live in a tepee. Said she'd jump in the river and drown before she'd ever be with a man that'd make her do those things. Said she was a woman of independence."

"What'd you say?"

"Hell, I fell down on the floor laughing."

"You seem to take rejection well enough."

"Me and Jane could have been happy, even though I couldn't understand her half the time. She put a lot of stock in reading books."

"She wants to see me, huh?"

"Yeah. I don't think she's got long to wait."

"You go on back and tell her thanks for the supplies."

"You want me to say you're coming?"

"Just tell her thanks."

"You don't show, I'll tell her I found you dead and buried you—that way she won't be hurt too much that you didn't come."

Ben Moon watched as the Indian stood up slowly and adjusted his hat before stepping off the porch and over to the wagon.

He noticed how the Blackfoot walked on the balls of his feet—carefully, softly, as if he were tracking somebody. Like a white man, maybe, back in the old days when the Blackfeet were still free men and the white men were something to be tracked.

The spring wagon groaned under the Indian's bulk as he lifted himself up into the seat and took hold of the reins.

He looked back just once, saw the gaunt man standing in his union suit and bare feet, a faded blanket draped across his shoulders, standing on the porch of a raggedy Chinaman's shack. *Ben Moon,* famous gunfighter. How could a man sink so low in life, the Blackfoot mused as he snapped the reins across the rump of the gray.

Ben Moon watched from the porch until the spring wagon bumped out of view.

"Damn it to hell," he thought to himself. "Spring's come again and I'm still alive and Jane's dying!"

"Jane's dying!"

"Jane's dying!"

He tried to swallow down the words but only tasted his own bile.

Two

It seemed she had been dying a long time.

The winter had been hard—a visitation of evil that had racked her body with the bloody cough. The cold had been so terrible. So cruel.

She looked about her now—her room warmed by the shaft of sunlight that angled through the large window and crept across her bed. Her pale hands pressed into the bed cover, a quilt of red and black squares.

The illness had stolen more than her health. Sassy had been in earlier to brush her hair and rouge her cheeks and help dress her in a fresh nightgown.

"Bring me my mirror," she had requested. Sassy's mahogany face frowned. "I said bring it."

"Now, Miss Jane, why fuss? You're as pretty as you ever was."

But Sassy had brought her the mirror none the same, forced to by those stern green eyes that had lost their gaiety but not their fire.

She held the tortoiseshell mirror in both hands, unsteadily but with determination.

There was, in that first brief examination, the reflection of a woman much too old: The hair, once the fiery redness of autumn leaves, now dulled and laced with threads of silver; the sallow skin tinged yellow like old candle wax; the pale, thin lips that seemed bloodless, totally bloodless.

She placed the mirror face down on the quilt and looked at Sassy.

"There is no need to lie," she said simply.

Sassy started to shake her head—"Oh, no, Miss Jane"— but was cut off with a wave of the sick woman's hand.

"Bring me my best dress, girl."

The young woman hesitated, unsure of the order.

"It's in the dressing trunk. . . . Bring it to me." The cough took her mid-sentence. It shook her as though she were being shaken by some great, invisible force. Sassy stood mute, watching, waiting for the coughing to subside. It was terrible to see Miss Jane like this.

She remembered so easily nights in the big house with old Tink playing the piano downstairs and all the men and all the gay ladies having the best old time, as they did about every night in the big house—except for Sunday night, which Miss Jane had set aside for a time for the girls to have to themselves.

Miss Jane wasn't religious, at least she didn't ever say that she was or pretend to be. She didn't go to church either—said the town ladies would run her off if she ever was to. All that fire in Miss Jane's green eyes sparked up whenever she talked about it.

"Mine is the finest parlor house in the territory. My girls are pretty and my whiskey not watered. Here, their men can get a fair shake, clean sheets, and honest whores. What in the world do those women expect of me?"

It would always put Miss Jane in a blue mood whenever the subject took hold of her. She would sulk for hours afterwards.

It was true enough, Sassy had thought. Miss Jane ran a

good house. Clean and neat. She made the cowboys scrape the mud from their boots and insisted they not spit their tobacco juice on the carpet. And they had to be polite to the girls and not abuse them, or else they didn't come back. Miss Jane insisted on such rules.

And in exchange, all the gents who abided could expect no trouble in return. Miss Jane had hired Ned Bluecorn to make sure that everyone behaved themselves. Sassy thought Ned Bluecorn was the vilest man that ever took a breath. Mean and ugly and smelly. But, he was tough, too.

He brooked no ill-behavior from any of the customers, tolerated no open drunkenness, cursing, or loaded weapons within the big house. Sassy feared him, but Miss Jane tolerated him and paid him good wages and let him sleep in a room off the kitchen.

He followed Miss Jane around like a big hound.

On Sundays, Tink always fixed a big meal and served it around a long oak table he'd pull out of the storeroom and set up in the parlor, and all of them would sit down like regular family and eat and laugh and talk and drink fruit wine . . . and it was just the best time.

She saw how the linen hanky stained red when Miss Jane coughed into it. *Oh, Lordy, she don't have the blood to spare.*

There was a heavy knock at the door. Sassy nearly jumped out of her skin.

"Who's there?" she managed after taking in a sharp breath.

"You let me in, Sassy." It was that ugly old Indian, Ned Bluecorn, his voice so deep it sounded as if he were talking from the bottom of a well.

"You go on and come back later," Sassy said shrilly.

"No, let him in," said Jane.

"He stinks, Miss Jane. Smells like turpentine and horse sweat."

"Let him in, Sassy."

He stood there, the big old goose, filling up the doorway his dark ugly eyes coming to rest on her like those of a vulture looking down on some weak helpless creature which was the way Sassy felt whenever in Ned Bluecorn's presence.

Sassy recalled when Miss Jane had told her how Ned Bluecorn had asked her to marry him—right after she first took sick with the cough. It had made her squirm just to hear Miss Jane tell about it.

Sassy shrank from the door as Ned Bluecorn entered For such a big man, he walked easy.

"You look pretty good today," he said, his gaze shifting from Sassy to Jane.

She looked past him to the square of window light and then back again.

"It seems we have our first pretty day," she said, smiling enough to show even, white teeth.

"Almost too warm too quick," he replied. "Ice is breaking up in the river already."

He held his big, black felt hat in both brown hands: held it like a schoolboy waiting to be dismissed or invited to si down, whichever came first.

"Well?" she said.

He pretended that he didn't understand the question.

"Well, did you go out there and see Ben Moon or didn you?"

"Yeah, I went out there."

"Was he drunk?"

"No."

"Dead?"

"No. He wasn't dead neither."

"Then I take it you talked to him?"

"Yeah. We drank coffee and smoked some cigarettes and talked for a while."

"Did you tell him I'd like him to come and see me?"

The Indian shifted his weight from one foot to the other. It was true, Jane had to admit, Sassy was right: Ned smelled bad.

"He didn't say if he would. He just told me to tell you thanks for the grub."

She felt the stab of disappointment even though she had told herself time and again not to be disappointed. Ben Moon was the most unpredictable man she had ever known.

"He don't seem in such good shape himself," said Ned Bluecorn. "He seemed pretty old and worn out, wore a blanket around himself the whole time I was there and shivered like a wet dog."

Whatever happened to who we were? she asked herself.

"Sassy, did you find my dress yet?" Sassy had spent the whole time staring up at Ned Bluecorn as if he were some twisted old tree ready to fall down on her.

"Yes, Miss Jane. I was just now doing that."

She moved toward the trunk in the corner of the room but did not take her eyes off the Blackfoot, fearing that if she did, he would grab her and carry her off. Lord only knows what a man like Ned Bluecorn might do, especially to some young black child like herself. She had heard once from a cousin that Indians ate people—and that Blackfoot Indians in particular would pluck out your heart and eat that first and then eat the rest of you for dessert.

It made her shudder, and it felt as if insects were crawling up her back every time he looked at her.

"Ned, I want you to fix me a bed up in the wagon."

He didn't need to ask her why.

Even though he had lived around them for nearly twenty years, had learned to eat potatoes and wear shoes and sit in a chair, he still could not figure out entirely how the minds of white people worked.

"You going out to see him? You going out there?"

"Yes," she said, those bloodless lips barely moving so that her voice came out like a whisper. "I want you to take me out there to see Ben."

"Miss Jane . . ." He knew it was pointless to try and talk her out of doing what she planned. It escaped him, her ongoing interest in Ben Moon.

"Whatever it is you want him to do for you, Miss Jane, I can do it just as well—and sober!"

Her gaze came to rest on him, to dwell, to stare at him until he shifted his weight again.

"I know you could, Ned. There are things you don't understand."

"Because I'm Blackfoot? Because I'm Indian and he's a white man?"

"I don't think of you as an Indian, Ned—not a man who's worked for me as long as you have. Not a man who asked me to marry him once."

He saw the faint smile and it made her beautiful again.

"Go get the wagon ready for me, will you, Ned? I'll need my privacy now while Sassy helps me to get dressed."

For a time, he did not move. She was the most beautiful white woman he had ever seen and, even now, in her sickness, she still captivated him.

"Well, go on, you big ol' thing. You heard Miss Jane. Scoot! She has to get herself dressed to go calling on a gentleman!" This last Sassy said with a great deal of satisfaction, for the last thing ugly ol' Ned Bluecorn would ever be in his entire life was a gentleman.

Ned turned slowly like an old bull looking for a way out of his pen. Sassy waved her apron after him as though shooing him out or clearing the air of his scent.

It took most of an hour for Jane to get dressed. Several times, she had to halt her efforts and struggle with the terrible cough; and then she needed minutes more to regain her strength.

When at last she was dressed and sitting before the oak dressing table with its large oval mirror, she saw the faintest remnants of a younger woman, a woman of health and beauty and youth.

There, in the deepest portions of the green eyes where the splintered light still shone brightest, was the reflected portrait of Jane Marie Westlake.

How long ago had she been known as Jane Marie Westlake? Daughter to Av and Hazel Westlake of Boston. Debutante. Bride of Edward James Johnson candidate for governor.

Fragments. Mere fragments of memory and past that may not even have existed at all—so far removed from Lost River, Montana Territory.

"You okay, Miss Jane?" Sassy's voice broke her reverie. "Should I go get Tink to help us down the stairs?"

"Maybe so, Sassy. I feel as weak as a dish rag."

Sassy's skirts swished as she crossed the room. Jane watched in the mirror as Sassy turned the porcelain doorknob in her dark hand.

The brown girl nearly leaped out of her skin when she

opened the door to a tall, thin, shadowy figure standing there as still as a ghost.

"Lordy!" she gasped and staggered back a step.

Jane said, "I'm glad you could make it, Ben."

Three

The man stepped into the light of the room. Sassy's gaze was fixed upon him.

He was tall enough so that he had to bend slightly to enter the room—as tall as ol' Ned Bluecorn, but not nearly as heavy. He needed a shave. A shave and some fixin' and he'd prove to be a handsome man.

Even in the somewhat poor light, Sassy could see the man's colorless eyes that looked at her but didn't look at her.

He wore a pinch-crowned Stetson that could have used brushing and a long linen duster that came down to his boot tops. He looked as scrawny and battered as an alley cat and just as mysterious.

Sassy saw the way his gaze left her, drifted across the room, and came to rest on Miss Jane, who had half-turned in her chair in order to face the man.

"Jane."

The name came out like a low growl, but soft, like the sound that old alley cats have when they're content—or cross.

He saw the woman across the room nod her head slowly, as though approving. Of what, he could not guess. He must look a sight. The winter had been a hard and long one; and it had gotten too damn cold to wash himself, or his clothes, in the river anymore, and even when he tried and hung them out to dry, they froze as stiff as boards.

He should have shaved. He could have at least shaved. But the hands were unsteady and the razor sharp, and—hell—he most likely would have cut his own throat had he tried. Now, seeing that she was dressed and looking favorable, he felt self-conscious about his own appearance.

"Ben."

She seemed frail; he remembered a time when she hadn't been.

"You hungry, Ben? It looks like you could stand to eat."

"Do I seem that bad?" He rubbed the fingers of his right hand across the whiskered jaw.

He saw her smile, a reminder of how beautiful she could be when she smiled.

"Ned said you might not come. I was getting ready to come to you. I was looking forward to the fresh air. Ned's fixing up the wagon now."

"I reckon I could take you for a ride if that's what you'd want."

"You're not obligated."

"I reckon I wouldn't see it as an obligation," he said. It seemed to please her.

"Lord, I guess fresh air would do me fine. Sassy, bring me a cape, the blue one."

"You sure you ought to be goin' out, Miss Jane?" As she had done with Ned Bluecorn, she hadn't taken her eyes off Ben Moon. One was bad, the other worse, at least as far as she was concerned.

She had heard talk about Ben Moon; plenty of talk. It was said he was a man-killer and wanted in Texas and Arizona, that he was quick with a gun and would shoot a man without hesitation.

'Course, standing there looking at him now, she couldn't see none of that in him. He just looked like some broken-down old tramp come by the house for a handout.

Still, he had those cold, empty eyes that'd probably seen all a body could imagine. Miss Jane seemed to favor him, though. Always had, as far back as she could remember.

When Miss Jane came to Lost River five years back, it didn't seem no time at all before Mr. Ben Moon showed himself up riding a big ol' blood-bay horse and looking like the Avenging Angel, the way he'd stare down at a body with those icy eyes of his.

Miss Jane had said after Mr. Ben Moon had shown himself that first time that the two of them went way back together. Miss Jane had told her that they had first met in Abilene, Kansas, years ago and had known each other ever since. Miss Jane had said that, back in those days, Ben Moon was a lawman and that he had a famous reputation.

Staring at him now, Sassy did not doubt for a moment that Ben Moon was a man with a dark past. One that she hoped never to learn the truth about.

"Sassy, why is it that I have to ask you everything twice this morning?"

"Huh?"

"I asked you to please get me a shawl so that I may go for a wagon ride."

"Yes'm, if that's what you want, that's what I'll get you."

Ned Bluecorn looked more than a little disappointed when he saw Ben Moon and Jane descend the wide staircase together. He had made a bed of blankets in the spring wagon and had brought it around front when he'd noticed the man's blood bay tied up to the hitch rail. The horse was as raw-boned and rank looking as its owner.

Ned Bluecorn's dark face twitched at the sight of the two

of them together. It twitched more when he saw that Ben
Moon had a hand supporting her elbow.

"Thank you for fixing up the wagon, Ned. I won't need
you to drive me. As you can see, Ben's arrived. I've asked
him to take me for a ride so that I can taste the sweetness
of the air and feel the sun upon my face."

The eyes of the Blackfoot met with those of the white
man and, in that instant, something unsaid was spoken between them.

"I could ride along, if you want," said Ned Bluecorn.

"It won't be necessary," said Jane.

"I don't mind. I don't mind at all."

"No," she said, shaking her head. "There are things I
need to talk about with Ben. Private matters."

He stood blocking the door for a moment, his wide shoulders nearly touching the frame on either side.

"I didn't think you'd show," he said, his dark eyes ex-
pressing his disappointment.

"You mean you hoped I wouldn't," said Ben Moon.

There were more unspoken matters between them, matters delivered and received in the unflinching gazes of each.

"I just didn't think you would," the Indian said finally
and stepped aside.

"Where to?" Ben Moon asked her after she was in the
bed of the wagon, properly propped up and resting on a set
of woolen blankets.

"Let's ride out to Elk Meadow. It's always been a favorite
spot of mine." He snapped the reins across the rump of the
gray and "hawed," and the wagon rattled to a start.

He drove slowly, trying to avoid the ruts and bumps in
the road, a road slick with thawing mud.

To her, everything seemed a wonderment, as though she

were seeing everything for the first time. It had seemed so long, the winter.

They rode for a time like that: Him, studying the rump of the gray as it walked along; her, taking in the sweep of hills, the stands of trees that lined their slopes, the clear blue sky that seemed endless, the distant snow-capped mountains.

Eventually, they arrived at a meadow. Remnants of a split-rail fence bordered one side of it. Aspens stood tall along its edges. She thrilled to see it again.

He spread the blankets on the ground and helped her to them.

"Do you mind if I smoke?" he asked.

She did not mind.

She watched him smoke, staring off in different directions as though expecting something to happen. Sitting there, looking up at him, she thought he looked as tall and lean as one of the aspens.

"Are you warm enough?" he asked.

"Yes."

"I had this filled at the saloon," he said, pulling a metal flask from his pocket and holding it forth. "Do you care for a drink?"

She looked uncertain.

"It's peach brandy. It's just a little something to warm you on the inside."

She smiled and reached a hand for it.

He watched as she sipped it. Tentatively, like a child tasting something for the first time. It made her cough, but only slightly. She waited for its full effect before handing it back to him.

"Yes," she said as he took the container from her. "It's warm and wonderful."

He tilted the flask to his own lips and swallowed.

She watched a yellow bird with black wings fly from tree branch to tree branch. He saw it, too.

"Thank you for bringing me here, Ben."

"Ned said you've been sick most all winter."

"More than sick, Ben."

He didn't want to say it. He didn't want her to say it.

"I reckon you're smart enough to have seen a doctor."

"I saw two. Why don't you sit down next to me?" It seemed to take a great bit of effort for him to do so. He sat cross-legged still staring off at something out beyond them.

"I'm dying, Ben. There's no getting around it." For the first time since leaving the big house, he looked directly into her eyes.

"It seems hard to believe," he said.

"What, that I'm dying?"

"Yes. That and the fact that we've lasted this long."

"It doesn't seem like much," she said. "We're given so little time. I never, before last autumn, even thought about dying; and now here it is upon me, and it is all that I *can* think about."

She watched him pull cigarette makings from his shirt pocket, watched as he tapped the tobacco into a paper and rolled it and flicked his tongue over it before striking a match to it. Then, taking a finger, he flicked off a piece of loose tobacco from his lip and blew a haze of smoke that danced in the wind and was gone.

All the while, his eyes rested everywhere but on her.

"Will you ever find your peace, Ben Moon?" she asked. Then the eyes came round and rested on her.

"I'm okay with the way things are, Jane," he said. "It

may not be the best of life, the way I'm living now, but it's not the worst, either."

"I remember a time when you cut a dashing figure. Now, look at yourself."

He rubbed the stubble of his chin. "I should have shaved."

"It's got nothing to do with shaving," she said.

"What in the world are you talking about, Jane?"

"I just hate to see you this way, Ben. You look broken down and used up, and you're not even forty years old."

"Turned forty last winter—December, I think."

"Damn you, Ben Moon! Why is it you have never taken me seriously in all the years we've known one another?"

His eyes lowered from hers and studied the cigarette he held between his fingers.

"Never thought there was a need to get serious with you, Jane. We were always good times whenever we were together. Have you forgotten that?"

"No. No, I haven't forgotten what we were. Trouble is, we were really never anything to each other. We could have been. I would have married you. You were the *only* man I would have ever married."

He took a deep drag on the cigarette and blew the smoke out slowly.

"There was a time when I considered asking you," he said, bringing up his gaze to meet hers once more.

"I doubt it."

"Believe what you will. But I thought hard on it once."

"Well, that's the damned nicest thing you've ever said to me, if it's true."

He shoved back the brim of his hat and grinned at her. "You sure are a woman with grit. I'll give you that."

She returned the smile.

"Even as run down as you are," she said, "you can still be a handsome man when you smile."

"Now, Jane, don't go to flattering me; it'll just ruin my disposition." For the first time in a long while, she laughed. She had always loved that about Ben Moon: He could make her laugh.

The laughter broke into coughing. Her body shook with it. He encircled her with his arms and held her until the wretched spasms subsided. He noticed then how thin-boned she felt to him, how frail.

Neither spoke for a time. It felt okay to him that neither said anything, that he could simply hold her and that she rested her head upon his shoulder.

"They say that women like me wind up either poisoning themselves or marrying rich men or dying of the consumption," she whispered. "I guess whoever said that knew what he was talking about."

"It's dark talk for the woman I knew you to be," he said.

"I'm not the same woman I used to be any more than you're the same man you used to be," she said.

"No, I reckon you're not."

"I was wondering this morning whatever became of us, Ben? It seems like no time at all has passed, and yet there is no time left to us. You've grown old before your time and . . ."

He wanted to take his knife and cut the sickness from her body and draw all the sadness out of her as he might have treated a snakebite. He wanted to sit in that meadow with her until she became well again.

He would have gladly traded places with her. She seemed to him the better of the two.

"There's something I want of you, Ben."

He couldn't imagine what.

"I want you to do something for me that I'd trust no other to do."

"You're right about me, Jane. I ain't much anymore. I ain't what I once was. I'd be willing to do anything for you, but I'm not so sure I'm up to the task. If there's someone else you could ask, you might better know that what you need doing will get done."

"There is no one else. Not for this there isn't." She touched his arm, rested her hand there. Her fingers rubbed the worn fabric of his coat sleeve.

"I want you to find my daughter," she said. She saw the faint trace of surprise in his eyes; he was not a man to show his thoughts easily.

"Didn't know you ever had a child, Jane."

"It was a long time ago," she said. He saw the flinching hurt in her eyes as she said it.

"I left her with some good people in Kansas to raise. I was young and had no man. I figured it was best for her to grow up in a family. . . . I figured—"

He placed a rough hand atop hers.

"You don't have to explain your reasons to me, Jane. I'm not judging you."

"You ought to know," she said. She told him about it. About the baby that had been named Sarah and the family and the years of separation and the money she had sent regularly and the correspondence she had maintained with the husband and wife.

"Up until a few months ago. Then, the letters stopped altogether. I've not lived a righteous life. Maybe I'm paying the wages of my sin. But I want to see that child more than anything else in the world before I die."

For the first time, he saw her cry. Small, thin trails of

wetness stained her sallow cheeks, and she bit the inside of her quivering mouth to ward off more.

"You don't have to hold up for me, Jane. You want to bawl, you go right ahead." And, she did. For a long time. And when she had stopped, she said: "I'll pay you five hundred dollars to find her and bring her to me."

"Jane—" This time it was her turn to cut him off.

"Don't put up a fuss with me, Ben Moon. First off, I'm not a poor woman; I can afford to pay you. Second of all, you could stand to get back on your feet again; the money would do that for you. It'd be the same as if I were paying you to do any other job. I have more money if you need it, but I consider five hundred to be a fair price. The rest I want her to have."

"Why me, Jane? Why not Ned Bluecorn? He's been as much a friend to you as I have. Maybe more so. He asked you to marry him."

"Ned's a good man in his own right," she said. "He'd do it if I asked him. But, I want you to go."

"Why?"

The yellow bird with black wings returned and perched atop an aspen limb and cocked its head then let loose a sharp trill.

"Maybe it's because I always did love you and I need you to go and find the only other person I ever loved. Maybe, if you will do it, I'll know that you loved me, too. Don't make me try and explain it and sound silly."

He thought about the cabin and the two blankets and the ice breaking up on the river. He thought about other days and how the whiskey had made him feel when there had been enough of it.

She was asking something of him he wasn't sure he had to give.

He reached for his makings and discovered he had smoked the last of the tobacco. He unscrewed the top of the flask and tilted it to his lips, but then disdained the act and simply held it in his right hand.

"Will you do it?" she asked.

"What if I'm not able to?" he countered.

"You won't know that until you try."

He rubbed the stubble on his chin. "I sort of have liked my life the way it's been lately," he said.

"What? Lying out in that shack of yours, staying drunk and hungry most of the time? Keeping to yourself? How could you enjoy a life like that?"

He couldn't explain it to her. He couldn't explain the need to be alone, to be left alone.

"You're asking a lot of me, Jane."

"I wouldn't if it weren't important to me."

She coughed. He saw the red-tinged phlegm staining the white handkerchief.

"I'll leave in the morning," he said. "If that's all right."

"I half-expected you to say no. Why didn't you?"

"Hell if I know. What would you have done if I had said no?"

She chewed the inside of her lip, her green eyes searching his face.

"I guess I would have told myself one more time just how disappointed you've made me."

"Maybe you've always expected too much of me, woman."

"Maybe too little."

Four

"I want you to follow me up the hill," she said.

"Whatever for?" the man asked.

"For the reason I sent for you."

He studied the woman's features. She was as plain as paint. A full-bosomed woman in a calico dress and hair combed straight back and pinned up in a bun. He looked around the parlor they were sitting in.

Everything seemed neat and tidy.

He watched as she retrieved a shawl from a peg on the wall and draped it over her shoulders.

"Follow me," she said.

He walked behind her as she ascended a hillock a hundred yards from the house. She carried a handful of wildflowers and hummed a low sound of an old hymn he had heard before but could not remember the name of. She seemed a damn strange woman.

Reaching the knoll of the hill, they came to a small white picket fence surrounding a small graveyard. Inside the fence stood two headstones; one was more weathered than the other.

He watched as she opened the gate of the fence and knelt by one of the headstones placing the handful of flowers on the sunken place of the earth there.

"Mr. Sam Pepper has arrived, Charley," she said.

The man felt a slight chill crawl up the back of his neck. A sudden blow of cold wind ruffled his hair.

"I promised I'd send for someone to take care of our business, Charley, and now I have."

Still kneeling, she turned her attention to the man.

"This is my boy Charley, Mr. Pepper. All that's left of him, anyway." She returned her gaze to the ground, straightened the stems of the flowers to a more orderly fashion.

"I guess I ain't getting it," said the man.

She pressed a hand to the cold slab of headstone, her fingers tracing out the letters: Charley Duvall . . . Born 1868 . . . Died 1887 . . . Beloved Son . . . We Will Meet Again In Heaven.

Damned if he weren't about to turn around and leave when she spoke again.

"It's him, the reason I wrote for you to come. I asked people whom I should send for. I asked Jute Walters down in town. Jute served time in the penitentiary for armed robbery. I asked him who there was I could send for to avenge my Charley's murder. He told me you would kill a man for a price. I asked him was he sure. He said as sure as he was of anything. He said you was known all over Colorado as a manhunter. I looked at that old man in his eyes and made him promise, made him swear he was telling the truth. He swore it."

"I reckon that man told you right," he said.

"Then I am glad you have come."

"You said in your letter that you'd pay expenses as well as my fee for coming. My fee is five hundred dollars if I take the job you offer me."

"You didn't waste your time coming, Mr. Pepper. I'll see to that."

"I'll need a portion of the money right off. I'll collect the rest when the job is finished."

"That won't be a problem, Mr. Pepper. Not if you're up to the task, it won't."

"Ma'am, I know my abilities."

"Good, walk with me back down to the house. Do you drink tea?"

She poured him tea from a silver pot into china cups whose handles were too small for him to get his finger through. He sweetened his with four spoonsful of sugar. She looked amazed.

"You seem a refined man, Mr. Pepper, for someone in your line of work."

"Don't know so much about refined, Mrs. Duvall, but I have gone to the opera a time or two and have eaten oysters right out of the shell."

"Can you read or write?"

He found her conversation to be boring and irrelevant to the matter at hand.

"Yes, ma'am, I can. And I can cipher, too, if that's your next question."

"I can see you are an impatient man, Mr. Pepper."

"Yes, ma'am. I tend to be."

"Then I suppose we should talk about my Charley."

"It ain't necessary. I won't be tracking your boy, ma'am. I'll be tracking the man who killed him."

"It's important that you first know about Charley," she insisted. He bit the inside of his cheek to keep from speaking his mind. He could use the money, if she truly had any. And although she had thus far paid in advance, his expenses involving the trip out from Denver—just as he had demanded in his wire—he doubted seriously as he looked around the plain, simple frame house that she had five hundred dollars.

He'd give it a few more minutes.

She showed him a tintype in a silver frame. The image was a youth with slicked-down hair dressed in a checked suit, his right hand resting on a table, a nickel-plated pistol in his left. The boy seemed pleased with himself, with his pose.

"That's Charley. It was taken the same year he was murdered."

Sam Pepper sipped his tea and waited patiently for her to continue a story he had little interest in.

"I wanted him to become a doctor like his late father. He said he wanted to become famous. I didn't want him to have that gun. He wouldn't listen to me."

The woman's face bunched and reddened. He averted his gaze. He had no need to watch a woman cry.

"Charley was wild, I'll admit. And that damn gun didn't help matters any. He'd practice with it day after day. It hurt my ears to hear him shoot it so much."

Sam Pepper pulled the Elgin watch from his pocket and studied the time. He did it with intent. He did it until she took notice.

"He was shot down in a saloon!"

"That's why I've come, Mrs. Duvall. To find the man that shot your Charley and see to it he is avenged." Finally, they had gotten to the matter at hand.

"Yes, Mr. Pepper. That is why I have sent for you."

"Then, we are agreed?"

"Yes. Yes."

"You don't have kin that can do it for you. Your husband has passed, and you need to know that justice has been seen to."

"Yes. Yes, Mr. Pepper. You have understood."

"Completely, Mrs. Duvall. That is what I do. I understand folks need to see that justice is served where the law cannot."

"Especially so in this matter, Mr. Pepper, for it was a lawman who murdered my Charley."

Well, now, that was a piece of news he hadn't counted on.

"How so, Mrs. Duvall?"

"A man named Ben Moon." She saw the man across from her stiffen slightly at the mention of her boy's killer.

"Do you know him?"

"I have heard of him, yes, ma'am." There was more truth in it than what he told her.

She studied the man Sam Pepper for a long full moment: Dark, deep-set eyes; thinning dark hair that stuck close to his head where his hat band had pressed in; a long face, not unhandsome; tall and thin of frame, long-limbed; good clothes.

"You hardly seem what you represent yourself to be, Mr. Pepper."

He shrugged his shoulders slightly.

"I reckon not many people seem what they are just by looking at them."

He looked to be about forty years of age.

"This man, Ben Moon," she said. "What have you heard about him?"

"Well, he has made himself a reputation as a gunfighter, a man that does not go far out of his way to avoid trouble." He paused, sipped some of the sweet tea from his cup. It had grown tepid.

"The sort of man that would kill your boy if your boy was to give him trouble," he said.

She thought to herself that Mr. Sam Pepper could just as well be describing himself. She noticed that the tip of the little finger on his right hand was missing and that a slight scar revealed itself just at the corner of his mouth where his mustaches hung heavy and long.

"What makes you think you could stand up to such a man, Mr. Pepper?"

"I don't plan on standing up to him, Mrs. Duvall."

"Well, how then . . ."

"I don't plan on it being a gunfight where we face each other down on some street," he said, a slight smile playing on his lips.

"I guess I don't understand," she said.

"It's simple. You pay me to kill him; I kill him. It doesn't matter how."

"Oh, I see."

They sat for a time, the stillness of the room enveloping them both. A Regulator clock ticked a steady rhythm. He stared at the flocked wallpaper while she stared at him.

"You should know," she said. "My boy Charley lingered for a long time before he died—nearly a year. He was crippled from where the bullet shattered his spine. He couldn't eat nothing and keep it down."

Sam Pepper tried one of the tea cookies the woman had placed on a small china plate in front of him. They were sweet.

"He was like an infant the whole year. I had to change him and make him wear a diaper because he couldn't control himself. He cried and was in pain all the time. It was pitiful what my boy had to go through."

"Yes, ma'am, I think I know what you mean."

She looked not much older than he was himself. She had a long, pale face maiden-like. Her eyes were large and tired looking, like that of a hound. She had little chin. He did not find her attractive even upon close examination.

"He died of peritonitis, my boy Charley," she said, staring up at the ceiling. "Lord, how he suffered!"

"Would you like to go into the bedroom with me?" he asked.

"What?" she repeated.

"I just thought you might be lonely after all this," he said.

"Don't be foolish, Mr. Pepper. And, don't forget why you are here."

He shrugged his shoulders again.

"No, ma'am. I haven't forgotten."

"Then I expect if I am to hire you that you will be willing to sign a contract as to the terms of our agreement."

"No, ma'am, we won't sign any agreements."

"Then how am I to know that you won't take what money I give you and just ride off?"

"You are a damn strange person," he said.

"I am a woman who grieves for her son. I am also practical."

"You want to sign contracts, you hire a lawyer. You want to hire me, there'll be no contracts other than what we shake hands on."

She sighed, touched the face of the cameo brooch she wore pinned to the bosom of her dress.

"How will you find Ben Moon, after so much time has passed?" she asked.

"I have my ways," he said. "The Ben Moons of this world are easy to find. Where do you suppose men like that can go and not be noticed?"

She thought his smile sinister. It made her uncomfortable

to have him look at her the way he had ever since their return from Charley's grave.

"I agree to pay you half the money now, the other half payable when you have . . . finished. I will require a newspaper account of Mr. Moon's death to confirm the event."

"Sure, sure." He stood. She thought the top of his head might touch the ceiling. He loomed over her, staring down at her.

"Are you certain?" he asked.

"About what?"

"About going in there with me?" His head tilted toward the open door of her bedroom.

"I think the sooner you begin your journey," she said, "the sooner it will be completed."

He held out his hand. He had long, graceful fingers except for the missing tip of the little one on his right hand. The flesh of his hand was as smooth and cold as marble.

"I'll be back for the rest of the money," he said as he stepped from the porch and mounted the big bay horse he had tied up outside.

He smiled enough so that the corners of his dark mustaches lifted displaying large front teeth.

"Maybe I'll be back for more than just the money," he said.

"Don't trouble yourself with strange notions, Mr. Pepper. If I have enough money to hire you, I have enough to hire other men to take care and see that I am not troubled by the likes of you."

"Har!" he laughed.

"Har! Har!"

Later, long after he had ridden away, she sat beneath the Regulator clock and listened to it tick.

Five

He had bought whiskey in town, and tobacco. It was all a man truly needed.

He had sat that evening, smoking his cigarettes and drinking his whiskey and watching the sun melt beyond the mountains.

He could hear the cracking of ice breaking up in the river.

The air was sharp and biting, especially so after the sun went down. The whiskey warmed him.

Jane was dying. It was something he couldn't get out of his head. It played and played like words to a children's rhyme.

His knees ached from the cold, he had sat so long. And when he stood, it seemed difficult and hardly worth the effort.

You've gotten old, Ben Moon. Damn if forty years seems that old, but it sure feels like it.

It had seemed to have happened all at once, over the winter.

Something heavy flew overhead, wings flapping—an owl, perhaps.

Why did she have to be dying so soon?

Death was a sure thing. It was the one sure thing in life.

The one thing a man could always count on. He had been lucky so far. Or maybe not.

The sky had turned brassy; the distant mountains drew a black, jagged line against the brassy sky. The end of the day.

The whiskey nearly gone, he felt tired. He turned and went inside the small shack. Without bothering to light the oil lamp next to the cot or to undress, he fell upon the bed and waited for the demons to come.

He was awakened by the sense of someone standing in the room. With one hand, he shielded his eyes against the glaring light coming through both doorway and window. With the other hand, he reached for the three-pound pistol that he kept under his pillow.

"Whoa up, Ben! It's just me, Ned Bluecorn."

The pistol was already in his hand, already swinging up, already being cocked.

Ned Bluecorn ducked through the open doorway just as wood splintered from its frame. He fell face down in the slick cold mud and swore. "Jezzus Christ!"

Ben Moon had rolled off the cot and was on his hands and knees listening to Ned Bluecorn swearing like a miner. Leftover whiskey vapors and pieces of nightmares were still swirling around in his mind as he held the heavy Starr revolver in his hand.

He heard the high-pitched voice of a woman. "Lordy, Mr. Ben killed that ol' Indian! Lordy! Lordy!"

He lifted himself from the cold dirt floor and walked cautiously to the door.

Ned Bluecorn was standing there studying his mud-soaked clothes.

He saw Ben Moon and took a sudden step backwards.

"You ought to be more careful with that piece," sputtered the Indian. "You damn near shot the back of my head off!"

He turned his attention from Ned Bluecorn to the women in the spring wagon: Jane and the colored girl, Sassy.

Sassy looked as though her eyes might bulge out of her head.

Then, he realized she was exchanging stares between the muddy Ned and himself in his frayed union suit.

"Lordy!" she said.

"Is this some sort of farewell party?" he asked.

Jane sat in the wagon's bed, just as she had done yesterday, wrapped in heavy blankets, pillows propped up behind her.

He noticed the extra horses tied to the back of the wagon.

"You drink too much, Ben. You nearly killed Ned."

"Ned ought to be more careful whom he sneaks up on."

"I wasn't sneaking!" protested the Blackfoot. "I just come in to wake you."

"Maybe you should've knocked first."

"I did. I heard you snoring. I figured you was dead drunk."

"Well, what'd you come out here for?" he asked, returning his attention to Jane. "It didn't take the whole lot of you just to come and wake me up."

"We came to tell you we're going with you, Ben."

She saw the way he squinted his eyes at the announcement, the way the muscles in his jaws tightened under the bristle of old beard.

"We?"

"That's right."

"Who in the hell is we?"

"Me, Ned, and Sassy."

"Well, hell, why don't we just hire a marching band and maybe a circus to go along, too?"

He held the three-pound pistol in his right hand, still hung over and in his underdrawers, and wondered if maybe his life hadn't gone to cold ashes.

"Look at yourself, Ben Moon. Half-drunk and mean as a snake!" Jane's words came out in short, sharp bursts.

"I don't know whether I'm just plain mad or disappointed."

"About what?" he asked.

"About you! About the fact you're still lying around this shack dead drunk and worthless!"

"I ain't drunk, Jane!"

"Why else then would you be standing in your front yard in your drawers, waving a gun around at the only friends you have?"

He looked hard at the Indian.

"Do you mean you and Ned Bluecorn?"

"Yes."

"Hell, I don't recall the day when me and Ned ever became friends!" His feet were getting cold, but he didn't want to admit it. It was embarrassing enough that he stood before women in his ragged underdrawers.

"Well, like it or not, Ned's brought you food and looked in on you during the winter," she protested.

"Hell, he only came out here to see if I were dead so's he could steal my horse and saddle and all the other good things I own in this world!"

"You are being foolish," she said.

Sassy rolled her eyes in her dark face and whispered something to Jane. He couldn't catch it. Jane, in turn, patted the colored girl on the arm as though trying to comfort her.

"I can see now that my decision to go along to find my

daughter was the right one. You are in no condition or of a right mind to see the job through alone."

"Well, that is a damn insult!" he said.

"It isn't meant to be," she said.

"You are not up to the journey," he argued.

"Maybe not," she said. "I won't know until I try. But, I am as up to it as you are, judging by what I'm seeing."

"It wasn't our agreement," he said.

"Our agreement was that I pay you five hundred dollars to find Sarah. There was no talk, agreed or otherwise, as to whether I could or would come along. I've decided that I will."

"Then you'll go alone."

"We have an agreement, Ben Moon. Will you see it carried through?"

There it was, for the first time since he had seen her yesterday: The Jane he had known a long time ago, the one full of fire and grit and life.

"I agreed to go alone," he said. The whiskey had given him a big headache.

"Then you have misunderstood. If you will not hold up to your end of the bargain, Ned, Sassy and I will see it through. I release you from the agreement. You truly are a disappointment!"

Well, hell!

"Ned, please climb aboard and get us out of this man's yard," she ordered. The Indian offered a smile of satisfaction as he walked stiffly toward the wagon trying to avoid the cold wetness of his clothes.

"You won't get a hundred miles with that crew, Jane."

She turned to answer but was suddenly overcome with coughing, the knuckles of one hand white and bony as she gripped the sideboard of the wagon.

Ned sat patiently on the wagon seat waiting for her coughing to subside; Sassy attended her, stroking her hair and whispering: "It'll be fine, Miss Jane. It'll be fine."

They wouldn't get a hundred miles, he told himself. They'd get waylaid by road agents, thieves, or renegade Indians. And if desperados didn't get them, the journey itself would: Swollen rivers; a late snowstorm; a broken wheel. *Hell, and that was only the half of it!*

She stopped coughing. Ned gave one final show of teeth in his dark face and took the reins in hand.

"Hold on, Ned!"

The Indian's eyes narrowed.

She looked up from the hanky she held to her lips. Sassy looked up as well.

The wind blew through his underdrawers; it might snow. They all three waited for him to speak.

"I won't be known as a man that makes an agreement and then breaks it," he said at last.

"Then you'll go?" she asked.

"I reckon so. But, do I have to be happy about it?"

He saw her lift her face to Sassy and smile. Sassy only frowned. So did Ned.

"We'll wait for you while you get your things," Jane offered.

He went back inside the cabin and sat on the cot. His head hurt like blazes; his feet were cold, and he had no whiskey left. Outside were two women and a Blackfoot Indian waiting to be led to who knew where in search of a child—a young woman—none of them had ever seen.

He shook his head. Life for him had come down to this.

Six

They followed the road south to Rock Springs in Wyoming Territory and then sold the mules and wagon and bought tickets for the Union Pacific Railroad heading east.

Jane protested selling the mules.

"We'll buy another rig when we reach Kansas," said Ben Moon.

"Those are my favorite mules," said Jane.

"Can't be helped," said Ben Moon. "Train's faster than them mules."

She looked sad when the man who bought them led them away.

They waited on the platform with the stiff wind blowing at their clothes, and the air smelled of cinder and creosote.

A fat man in a gray-checked suit kept pulling a watch from his pocket and checking the time. Two soldiers lounged on a bench and sniggered and told jokes and spat tobacco juice between their toes.

Sassy kept one eye on the soldiers, who were keeping both eyes on her, and one on Ned Bluecorn, whose full attention was on Jane.

The soldiers grinned and spat and grinned some more.

They were daring in their behavior, which gave Sassy a small sense of pleasure but a tingle of fright as well.

Jane sat stoically as though she were waiting for something uneventful to happen.

Ben Moon squatted on his heels and smoked a cigarette.

Heavy dark clouds gathered in the sky threatening rain, or snow. They bunched up against one another like fat gray cattle.

Ben Moon removed his Stetson, wiped his hatband, and set it back on his head, adjusting it carefully, comfortably.

Two cowboys rode up the street on tall horses—rough trade with weathered faces and stark stares. They had fresh haircuts and their ears stuck out. And where the hair had been shaved off their necks and around their ears, their skin was as white as lard.

They rode slowly past the railroad station and stared unabashedly at the two women.

One said, "Look at that colored gal. She's as pretty as ribbons."

The other had taken more notice of Jane.

"She seems sort of blue," he said.

Ned Bluecorn cast a baleful stare in the direction of the two cowboys.

"Big sonofabitch," said one of the cowboys, the one who had noticed Sassy.

"Indian, looks like," said the other.

"Big sonofabitch for an Indian," said the first.

Their saddles creaked as they rode past; their horses snuffled and tossed their heads and worked the bits between their teeth.

Ben Moon stared down the twin steel tracks clear to where they seemed to join together in the wavering distance. No train. The stationmaster had said the train was due in at 10:15. Ben Moon reckoned it was near that but couldn't be sure.

He considered walking down toward town and having a drink. The more he squatted on his heels, the more he considered it.

"I reckon you're gettin' thirsty," said Ned Bluecorn, suddenly next to him.

"You read my mind."

"Whiskey's a bad thing," said Ned.

Ben Moon pushed the brim of his hat back and looked up at the Indian.

"Since when did you get righteous?"

Ned Bluecorn wore a black suit coat and trousers that barely touched the tops of his brogans. He wore a white shirt, only it was soiled from so many days of wear without change.

He looked like a damn white man with dark skin.

"Whiskey killed my brother and two uncles," said Ned. "It made them crazy, made them want to fight everybody. My two uncles got killed by a deputy over in the Bighorn country. They worked in a mill sawing lumber."

The thick rumble of thunder shuddered through the clouds but at some distance.

"They were drinking. They drank up all their wages all the time. Worked just to drink. The deputy shot them both on the same day at the same time. He said they were disorderly."

Ben Moon let the cigarette burn down fairly close to his fingers before he flicked it away.

"My brother, he got drunk and fell off his horse and broke his neck. One of my uncles who later got shot by the deputy found him. He said the crows had pecked out his eyes. Whiskey is a bad thing."

Ben Moon stood; his knees ached when he did.

"I'm going down the street and get a drink," he said.

"What about them?" demanded Ned Bluecorn.

Ben Moon looked first at Jane, then at Sassy. Sassy was still tossing sidelong looks at the two young soldiers.

"I reckon they'll keep until the train arrives."

"Maybe I ought to go along with you," said Ned Bluecorn.

"Suit yourself."

Ned walked over to Jane.

"He wants to go and have a drink," he said.

"Don't let him get drunk or forget to return," she said.

"What if he does?"

"I'll leave it up to you to see that he does not."

One of the soldiers had stood, stretched, and then, acting as though he were merely wandering about, moved close to where Sassy stood. When he did, she pretended not to notice.

"You and them all together?" the soldier asked after standing a moment or two next to Sassy.

He was tall and skinny, and freckles dotted his long nose. He had thick, bushy red hair that pushed out from under his kepi. His voice was twangy, like loose banjo strings. She thought he sounded a little like the parrot Miss Jane had once owned.

"Yes, we are," she said. "We's all headed for Kansas."

"What ya goin' there for?" he asked.

"My, but you're as curious as a cat," she said.

He glanced over his shoulder at the other soldier and grinned so wide all his teeth showed.

"Yes, ma'am, I reckon I am."

The boy flushed pink. She felt a bit of a flush herself. She was being daring—and with a white boy at that!

"You'd better move on, mister. Don't be fooling with these ladies." It was Ned Bluecorn, standing a good head higher and sixty pounds heavier than the soldier.

Sassy saw how the boy's face lost most of its color when

he looked up at the big ol' ugly Indian. Ned Bluecorn still wore his hair in braids. She reckoned it was so everybody would know he was still a *wild* Indian and not to be trusted or to be fooled with.

She saw how the young soldier's Adam's apple bobbed up and down in his throat as if it were trying to find a way out.

The soldier looked at his friend once, but the other soldier simply looked somewhere else.

The boy wanted to make a show of it; after all, it was nothing but a damn Indian ordering him off. But he could find no allowance in the Indian's gaze, no room. It was either fight or sit down. He touched the bill of his kepi and shuffled back to his friend.

"You ought to stay close to Jane," he said.

"Where's *that* devil goin' off to?" Sassy asked, pointing with her chin toward Ben Moon, who was already halfway down the street.

The two cowboys that had passed earlier walked their horses down the street again, as though they had little else to do.

Ned Bluecorn parted his coat just enough for the two cowboys to see the Smith & Wesson revolver he wore stuck inside his belt.

He saw them look at it and act as if they hadn't noticed.

"You stay with Jane, you hear me?" said Ned Bluecorn. His breath smelled like kerosene.

"That train comes pulling in before we get back, you run down to the nearest whiskey tent and get us," he ordered.

He stepped off the platform, caught a heel on a board, and nearly fell. She bit the inside of her cheek to keep from laughing.

It was a good thing she did: He gave her a dark stare.

Ben Moon was already inside the whiskey tent drinking a short glass of rye; it looked amber in the dull light.

The barkeeper looked up at Ned Bluecorn when he entered and said, "That boy's an Indian. We don't serve Indians."

He didn't say it in an ugly way. He simply said it as if he were reading it on a sign somewhere.

"He's with me," said Ben Moon without raising his gaze from the glass of rye.

"Don't matter who he's with. We still don't serve Indians. Goes for coloreds, too."

Ned stood at the bar.

"This man says he don't serve liquor to Indians," repeated Ben Moon.

Ned Bluecorn stared long and hard at the watery blue eyes of the man behind the bar.

"I don't drink," he said after a full minute. "Whiskey's bad for you."

The man looked relieved. He took his hand off the pick handle he kept behind the bar. It was a long piece of smooth hickory, heavy and hard. He thought it might take every bit of it to lay the big Indian low if he were to start trouble. He was glad he didn't have to mix it up.

"Why'd you tell Jane you'd do this?" asked Ned Bluecorn. Without waiting for an answer, he said: "I would have done it. She didn't need to ask you."

"I don't know why she didn't ask you, Ned. I told her I wasn't the one to do something like this."

"So why are you going to?"

Ben Moon studied what was left in his glass before drinking the rest of it.

"Don't press me, Ned."

There it was. Suddenly. That thing between them. That

temptation to have at one another, to prove once and for all who was the better man. Each man knew, instinctively, that if the fight were ever to come, it would be unyielding and without mercy.

Ben Moon placed a coin on the bar. "Another," he said. He sipped it as though it were hot.

Ned Bluecorn watched him carefully, as if he were watching a snake coil.

It wasn't hatred, what he felt toward Ben Moon. It wasn't fear, either. He wasn't like most white men, whose judgment and resolve were softer than their flesh.

Even standing there, drinking his whiskey, looking old and tired, Ben Moon was as dangerous as deep water. And just as unpredictable.

"This may end up bad," said Ned Bluecorn. "Our riding together."

"Possibly, Ned. Possibly."

"I still don't understand Jane's asking you."

"Let it drop, Ned."

"Maybe after we find Jane's daughter we should take care of this business between us."

Ben Moon grunted, swallowed the last of his whiskey, and set the glass down heavily atop the bar.

He turned slowly and looked up at the plain, simple face of the hulking Blackfoot. Indians were harder to read than a Chinese newspaper.

"The business between us isn't worth dying over, Ned."

"Maybe the way you see it."

The long blast of a train's whistle, followed by two shorter blasts, split the air.

"That'd be the ten-fifteen," said the barkeeper, pulling a nickel-plated watch from his pocket and checking the time.

"Yessir, on time as usual."

"Do you want a drink before we go, Ned?"

"You know I don't," said the Blackfoot.

"I just thought I'd ask," said Ben Moon, a slight smile playing at the corners of his mouth.

They stood amid chuffs of steam and waited for passengers to depart before climbing the three small steps up to their car. The train was like a great black beast shuddering beneath the gray Wyoming sky.

A man in a short-billed cap and ill-fitting coat asked for their tickets. They sat in red-velvet seats that faced one another. The velvet was worn thin and smooth in places. Jane and Ben Moon sat facing Ned Bluecorn and Sassy Sparks. They exchanged looks at first and then stared out of the windows at the now-empty platform.

A drummer with a large carpet-sided bag moved down the aisle and sat down across from them.

"How do," he said, touching the brim of his derby hat. He had a round red face and close-set eyes.

Sassy peered around the bulk of Ned Bluecorn and smiled brightly.

Ned gave her a dark look.

"Allow me to introduce myself. I'm Wilson T. Phiggs," he said, extending a soft, thick hand. No one offered to take it.

"Hmmm . . . well, yes," said the drummer after an uncomfortable time of holding his hand forth without its being shaken. He tapped his fingers on the carpetbag he held in his lap.

The train lurched and brought them all forward out of their seats, then lurched a second time, only not quite as much, and then was finally moving—slowly, but steadily—and the rail station slid out of view, then the town of Rock

Springs itself; and soon enough they were staring at the open, rolling landscape.

The drummer cleared his throat and said: "Are you folks going far?"

Ben Moon turned his head slowly, just enough to be able to look at the man directly. The drummer had the face of a man who had eaten a lot of pork in his time.

"I hope you're not going to talk all the way to Kansas," said Ben Moon.

The drummer started to reply, thought better of it, and busied himself with staring out the window on his side of the car.

The train had picked up its speed now, and they could all feel Wyoming slipping under their feet.

Seven

For the trip he had purchased a fringed buckskin jacket, a pair of calfskin boots, and a beaver hat. It would be cold in Montana, colder than in Texas.

He caught the stage north; and by the time he departed it in Cheyenne, he thought he might not ever be the same again. Two weeks of night-and-day traveling inside the coach—squeezed in between whiskey peddlers, bawling children, praying preachers, unkempt miners, and large women in sour smelling dresses—was about the worst experience he could recall.

The streets of Cheyenne were muddy from alternating days of rain and snow, spring weather for that part of the country. He tried hard not to get his new boots muddy, but it was impossible.

Cheyenne was as far as the stage went north. To go farther, he'd have to buy a rig.

He spotted a youngster leaning against a pole and called out, "Hey, boy, would you like to earn a quarter?"

The boy looked as if he ought to have been in a school classroom except he had the hard narrow gaze of a man and smoked a cigarette. He seemed to flinch at the question.

"Sure, mister," the youth said, looking at the man in the fancy buckskin jacket.

"Then carry my bag and rifle over to the nearest hotel."

The boy looked slightly baffled.

"You do have a hotel here, don't you?"

"We've got one, but it's usually full most of the time."

"Lead on anyway. And don't drop my Winchester in the mud."

He followed the kid across the wide swath of muddy street, dodging teamsters and men on galloping horses.

The Cheyenne House was a two-story structure of weathered pine. It had two balconies. He liked the looks of it. There were men lounging near the door and inside near the desk. They all gave him the eye as he passed.

He heard someone mutter, "Fancy son of a gun, ain't he?" He ignored it.

The kid walked to the desk and set down his bag and leaned his Winchester against the wainscoting.

"Well, ring the bell, boy." The kid looked peeved, but struck a hand down hard on the bell.

A clerk appeared—a slightly humped shouldered man with protruding eyes, eyes like a bull terrier.

He studied Sam Pepper from head to toe, then gave the urchin a hard look.

"I need a room," said Sam Pepper.

"We're full up," said the clerk.

"I'll pay extra if you'll move someone out."

"So will a lot of folks. Rooms are as hard to come by as chickens with teeth."

Sam Pepper looked at the kid.

"Is there anyplace else that has rooms in town?"

"This is the only hotel, mister."

"How about a boarding house?"

The youth hunched his shoulders.

"How much you willing to pay?"

"I'd go five dollars for a room."

"Just one night?"

"That's all I need; I'll be leaving in the morning."

He watched as the boy leaned down, picked up his bag and Winchester rifle, and said, "Follow me. I might know of something."

They walked clear to the west edge of town. His boots were slathered with mud, and even the knees of his trousers spotted from it. They walked until they came to a small, narrow, clapboard house that needed painting.

"You wait here a minute, mister. I'll go see what your chances are."

The boy disappeared inside the house and returned a few minutes later.

"She says she'll shelter you for the night but it'll cost you ten dollars."

"I said I'd go five."

"It's ten or sleep out in the streets, mister. It's probably goin' to snow tonight. It might be damn cold."

He saw the way the man looked at him without so much as even turning his head. He just moved his dark eyes was all.

"Well, I guess I'll have a look at that ten-dollar room you're offering," he said to the woman.

She hesitated. He reached inside his coat pocket, fingered through a brown leather wallet he carried, retrieved ten dollars, and handed it to her. She examined it briefly and then balled it up in her fist.

"This way," she said, walking down the hall toward the back of the house. "It ain't much."

It was a small room, hardly large enough for the bed which was a tick mattress held up by an iron frame and headboard.

"Blankets?" he asked.

"Jesse, go get Mr. Pepper some bed ware."

The boy looked crossly at his mother, but at the man's look sidled from the room.

"Jesse's reached the age where everything I tell him to do is a big chore."

He sat on the bed, tested it with his weight.

"I'd ask that you take off your boots before lying down," she said.

He allowed his gaze to rest on her for a long, full moment.

"I'm not ignorant," he said. "I'm not trashy."

"I didn't mean to imply anything," she said. "Just that these days, taking in boarders can be a risky business. The last one I put up stole some dishes. A cowboy from Texas."

"I don't suppose supper is included with the room," he said.

"I guess maybe I can set an extra plate." She leaned in the doorway, and the silver light coming through the window of the room caused her face to shine and her hair to shimmer.

"I don't suppose you'd take a walk with me later, after supper," he said.

"Don't get wrong ideas, Mr. Pepper. I'm not loose."

"Do you have a man?"

He saw how that struck her, the way she shifted her weight, the way the small muscles around her mouth tightened.

"You are very bold," she said.

"I'll admit to that," he told her, removing the beaver hat and hanging it on the back of a tall chair.

"I am widowed," she said.

"It looks like you've been a long time without someone," he said.

Her cheeks reddened, so did her neck. As he removed is jacket, she saw the pistol and gunbelt he wore. The grips f the pistol were pearl. She watched as he pulled a small erringer from his right boot and laid it under his pillow.

"Are you expecting trouble?" she asked.

"No," he said, removing his boots.

"I can't have trouble in this house, Mr. Pepper. I have a oy."

"No, no trouble," he said.

"Supper will be at six," she said as she turned to leave.

"What about that walk?" he asked.

Now it was her turn to study him. He had the sharp ngular features of a man who was impatient. There was n intenseness about him, a danger that shone through his tare. There was a certain grimness around his mouth and w, even when he smiled—as faint as that was.

"Perhaps," she said. Turning to leave, she paused once 10re. "Are you really a shootist," she asked, "like Jesse aid?"

"You know how young boys can be," he said. She took er leave and later knocked on the door at six sharp and nnounced that supper was on the table.

He washed in a pan of cold water—his face and hands. Ie worked some of the sleep out of his eyes with the knuck- s of his hands. Through the small window of his room e could see the fading light as day drifted toward night.

He had slept—two, three hours, he calculated. It took a ill moment to realize where he was when she knocked on 1e door. *Cheyenne.*

He tucked the derringer into his coat pocket and left the 1om.

The supper was plain. Boiled beef and potatoes and carrots. Plenty of carrots. He had to use lots of salt to put any taste into it. The kid had stared at him the whole time.

"I don't like to be looked at so much," he finally said, finishing the last of the carrots.

The boy blinked.

"No, sir, I didn't mean to stare, Mr. Pepper."

"I'd prefer that you not call me by my name, either."

Jesse Jordan swallowed hard, his mouth full of potato. It was an unusual request from a man, not to be called by his name.

He fell silent, embarrassed by the rebuke. He *had* hoped to curry the gunfighter's favor. *Hell, maybe even get a chance to shoot pistols with him.*

"Excuse me," he said, more to his ma than to the man. "I reckon I've had enough. I'm heading for town, ma."

"You'll just find trouble," she said. But he was already out the door, mad and stomping his feet as he walked up the muddy street toward town.

"He's difficult," she said, staring at the forkful of carrots she held in her left hand.

"A whipping might not hurt," he said, wishing there had been dessert—pie, maybe.

"He's too big to whip," she said. "Nor do I want to."

"Well, I reckon you'd know best," he said, pushing back from the table. "How about that walk?"

The evening air was cool and even with the heavy shawl she had draped about her shoulders, she felt chilled. But it felt good to have companionship, no matter.

He didn't say much, and they stuck to the dry parts of the street as much as was possible. He smoked a small black cigar as they walked, and she liked the smell of it.

"Where are you from, Mr. Pepper?" she asked.

"Colorado, mostly," he said. "Denver as of late."

"You are not a rancher or a cattle buyer," she said.

"No."

"Business brings you to Cheyenne," she said, drawing the shawl tighter still about her. She realized it was not *just* the night air that chilled her.

"Not to Cheyenne," he said. "Cheyenne is just a stop-over."

"Have you a wife? Children, perhaps?"

She saw by the way the glow of the cigar lit his face when he inhaled it that he was amused by her questions.

"Not that I know of," he said. He stopped, flipped the cigar to the mud, and ground it out with the heel of his boot.

"I'm only here for one night," he said. "I could stand some female companionship."

"You have misread me," she said. The dusk and the low brim of his beaver hat had hidden his face in shadows. She could see only fragments of light in his eyes.

"No," he said. "I have not. I am leaving in the morning, regardless of anything else. I have a job to do. I am only passing through. I would not like to spend tonight alone."

"You frighten me," she said. "Everything about you is dangerous and dark and mysterious. How can I consider such a proposal?"

"It's simple," he said. "You are alone; I am alone. To-morrow, we'll still be alone. We don't have to be alone tonight."

He was standing too close. She could smell his clothes, the scent of bay rum. Everything about him was wrong. She reached out and touched his arm just above the wrist. It was knotty and hard beneath the buckskin jacket he wore. He didn't pull away or move toward her. He stood, quiet and still, as a horse might.

"I have not been with a man in a long time," she said. "Any man."

"But you've thought about it," he said. "Thinking about it is something you can't ignore."

"You scare me," she said.

"It doesn't matter," he said.

He just stood there like a patient horse. She could not remove her hand from his arm.

"I don't want this to happen," she said.

"It'll be okay," he said. "It will all be okay."

Eight

Ben Moon stood on the open rear deck of the caboose and watched the great swells of prairie slide past.

The land this time of year was still brown and buff. The tall grasses laid over from winter like the combed-down hair of some great beast that lay sleeping or dead.

Come the spring rains, the grass would turn soft green and there would be cattle grazing on it and men upon horses and the smell would be sweet.

But now, gazing out upon its endlessness, Ben Moon could only sense a land that the winter had killed off. Even the distant mountains loomed black and void, except for where the snow lay upon them.

Black and white and brown is all that he saw from the rear deck of the rocking train.

Inside the third car forward sat Jane and Sassy and Ned Bluecorn. They could sit like that for hours, saying nothing, doing nothing, staring out the window—although Sassy would chatter until Jane asked her to please not.

He rested one hand upon the wrought-iron railing while he smoked a cigarette with the other. The pistol he carried in his side pocket lay heavy against his hip.

He thought about his shack and his place by the river and wondered if all the ice had broken up yet and if the river was flowing clear and cold and strong once more.

When he had first come to that place, he had stayed drunk most of the time. It had seemed worse than being locked up. But he stayed anyway. He knew he had to. His time as a gunfighter was over. A man grows old, no matter what. Old or dead. It sometimes seemed like one in the same.

Jane was right: He had gone to hell in every way a man could. But somehow, it didn't seem to matter much.

Ned Bluecorn joined him on the platform. The wind beat against his pant legs.

"I didn't think Kansas was such a long way," said Ned Bluecorn.

"It's a damn miserable long way, my friend."

"Jane's having a bad day," said Ned. "All this traveling and having to sleep sitting up has worn her out."

"Is she still feeling sorry for having sold the mules?"

"Yes. I think so."

"Women," snorted Ben Moon.

"You've loved her longer than me," said Ned.

"Well, that's a piece of news I haven't heard before," said Ben Moon, straightening up and flipping the cigarette over the railing of the car. It blew into sparks.

"She looks at you like you've loved her a long time," said the Blackfoot.

"I've loved lots of women in my time, Ned. Jane might have been one."

The train rounded a bend and they both leaned to the right holding to the handrail. Chuffs of black smoke passed overhead from the engine as it worked its way up an incline.

"She never did love me," said Ned, shaking his large dark head slowly. "She was the only white woman I could have lived with."

"Well," said Ben Moon, rubbing the small of his back

with a fist. "I guess we have all suffered rejection at one time or another."

The train had slowed considerably as it moved up the incline. Ned was about to say something when the train stopped altogether. It caused both men to lose their balance and grab the railing.

"There must be something wrong," said Ben Moon, peering around his side of the car. Looking up the line toward where the engine sat huffing great black billows of smoke, he could see men on horses.

"Damned if I don't believe we're being robbed!"

Ned Bluecorn looked, too, leaning over Ben Moon's shoulder.

Several men on skittish horses danced in and out of the black smoke. Some wore bandannas over their faces.

"Well, now what?" said Ned Bluecorn.

Before Ben could answer, some of the mounted men turned their horses and rode toward the rear of the train. Their guns drawn, they waved them at the staring faces framed in the windows of the passenger cars.

Ben Moon ducked back inside the caboose before any of the riders saw him. Ned Bluecorn did the same.

"Are we just going to let them rob us?" asked Ned Bluecorn as they worked their way forward to Jane and Sassy.

"Well, unless you think you can shoot it out with maybe a dozen armed men," said Ben Moon in a rough tone, "I guess so."

They found the women staring out the window. A man with a red bandanna pulled up over his face and riding a sorrel was staring back at them.

Jane said nothing, but Sassy was already carrying on.

"Lordy, we are being held up by bandits! They will kill us all!"

Ben Moon stepped forward and she shrank back.

"Put whatever money you're carrying inside your dress," he said to Jane. She looked at him, her eyes wide.

"Even trash like that won't body-search a woman," he said, nodding toward the window. "Do it quick!"

"What if they do?" cried Sassy. "What if they run their filthy hands all over us looking for valuables?"

"Then I kill whoever tries," said Ben Moon. He sat down in the seat opposite, tucking his pistol down in his boot and pulling his pant leg over it. Ned Bluecorn watched him, then followed suit.

Several men entered the car, their pistols drawn and held high for everyone to see.

They wore wide-brimmed hats that bent low over their faces; and with their bandannas pulled up, only their eyes were visible.

One of the men, a tall rangy fellow carrying a shotgun, shouted, "Stay calm, everyone. Don't give my boys reason to shoot!" Then he gave a horse-laugh and waved the barrels of the shotgun over the heads of the passengers.

Sassy was whimpering and covering her face with her hands. Jane sat passively as though she were watching a stage play. Ned Bluecorn's face grew dark and furtive. He had already determined that he would kill the first man to touch Jane.

Ben Moon felt an old feeling pass through him, one he had not had in a long time: Cold indifference to the threat of danger.

He watched the bandits move through the car taking money and jewelry and valuables from the passengers. He watched and waited for their approach—unafraid, undisturbed, prepared to draw the Starr from his boot and empty it into the faces of whoever might molest him, or Jane.

Unlike the dark and stormy countenance of Ned Blue-corn, Ben Moon's face was without a hint of concern.

The man with the shotgun stopped next to their seats.

He peered over the fringe of kerchief riding high on his nose, his gaze running over the four of them—first the men and then Jane and Sassy, then back to the men to see if they offered a challenge.

"Open up your purse, darlin'," the man ordered, motioning with the shotgun to the small silver-threaded bag Jane carried.

"I have only a few dollars," she said. "Would you rob me of that?"

"You're damn right, sister," said the man. "That and anything else you got, includin' that nice pin you're wearing." It was a cameo brooch.

She gave him the few dollars she had purposely left in the handbag and then removed the pin and handed that over as well.

He studied the small amount of money before stuffing it in his jacket pocket.

"How about you, colored gal?" he demanded, his wet, darting eyes shifting to Sassy.

"I ain't got no money, mister."

The man leaned forward across the erect Ned Bluecorn and jerked Sassy's clasped hands apart.

"Let me see," he persisted.

Jane said, "She's my traveling companion, my nurse. She has no money. She works for room and board."

The man turned his attention to Jane. The shift was sudden and rough, and Ned Bluecorn was reaching for the pistol in his boot when he looked into the eyes of Ben Moon. A barely perceptive flicker warned the Indian not to draw his piece.

The bandit's face was just inches from Jane's. She could smell his breath coming through the bandanna. He had been eating onions. After a long, tense moment, the man said, "You don't look so good, lady."

He straightened and brought his attention to bear on Ned Bluecorn. "You got money, Injun?"

Ned Bluecorn stayed focused on Ben Moon. *Why stop me from killing this man?* he asked with a look. But he knew why already. A dozen men or more were on the train with their guns drawn. It would be suicide.

"I asked if you had any damn money. Empty out your pockets." The man spoke in a loud voice, bringing the bead sights of the twin barrels to rest under Ned Bluecorn's chin.

Ned pulled his pockets inside out to show that they were empty. The man pressed harder with the shotgun and at the same time patted the Indian's other pockets. He found a pouch of tobacco and took that, then found a pocketknife and took that as well.

"I ought to shoot you for being so damn poor," said the man.

He studied Ben Moon and, for the briefest instant, their eyes met and locked. The man with the shotgun felt a stab of sudden uncertainty pressing against his spine as he looked into those clear, vacant eyes.

"Turn 'em out, mister," he said, but without authority.

Ben Moon turned out his pockets to show that they were empty but for the nickel-plated pocket watch and a few threads of lint.

The man shook his head, took hold of the pocket watch, studied it for a moment, and then dropped it into his own pocket.

"Damn poor pickin's," he said and moved on without further challenge to the man with the clear, vacant eyes.

Ned Bluecorn's face was a dark scowl. They had stolen his tobacco and pocketknife. But worse still, they had done it in front of Jane.

The robbers worked their way quickly through the car and then moved on to the next, leaving only one man to stand guard near the front.

"Well, ain't you gonna do something?" whispered Ned Bluecorn through clenched teeth.

"What'd you have in mind, Ned?" asked Ben Moon.

"There's only one of them now. I say we take the son-ofabitch. Bust his head open."

"Shut up the talk down there!" ordered the man standing guard. Ned Bluecorn looked up to see the man pointing his rifle in his direction.

In three more minutes, they were off the train. Sassy and Jane and Ned Bluecorn watched as the men jumped from the cars and struggled to mount their skittish horses, which were being held by a black man whose skin shone the color of wet ink under the glaring sun.

So busy were they watching the outlaws mount and make their escape that they failed to notice that Ben Moon had left his seat and exited the car.

He had stored the Henry rifle on a shelf in the caboose when they had first boarded the train—an old habit, storing weapons in different places. Now, he retrieved the gun and stepped onto the rear deck.

The gang had already cleared the tracks and were a hundred yards away, riding hard up a long slope toward a distant ridge.

Ben flipped up the rear sight of the Henry with his thumb and peered through it. He had not shot a man in a long time, especially not with a rifle.

The men were whipping their reins across the necks of

their horses. The animals' hooves threw up large clods of dirt and dead grass.

He took a deep breath, let it out slowly, took another, and held it.

One of the riders, the man that had taken his watch and Jane's brooch, came into view in his rear sight. Two hundred yards, maybe more.

He raised the barrel of the Henry slightly above the rider's hat to allow for the amount the bullet would drop in its travel. His finger squeezed the trigger—squeezed and squeezed until the rifle banged into his shoulder.

The rider rode on for what seemed another twenty yards, then pitched off his horse and flopped to the ground and did not move.

Ned Bluecorn saw the man drop just after he heard the gunfire from the rear of the train. Racing to the deck, he found Ben Moon, his rifle propped against the railing, making himself a cigarette.

The Indian looked out to the fallen man. He seemed a long way off.

The other riders had topped the ridge and had not stopped, nor turned back for their fallen comrade.

"That was a pretty good shot," said Ned Bluecorn.

"I think maybe it was," said Ben Moon, lighting his cigarette.

"The man that robbed us was riding a dun," said Ned Bluecorn. "I saw him mounting a dun. Was *he* riding a dun?" Ned pointed with his chin to the man that lay bunched in a heap on the dead yellow grass.

"He was," said Ben Moon.

"I think then maybe I will take back my pocketknife and tobacco," said Ned, a pleased look on his dark face. "Do you want me to get your watch while I'm at it?"

"Yes. And Jane's brooch. I'm sure she'd like it back."

The robbery had excited everyone, and so had the killing. The passengers swarmed off the train, eyeing the slope where the dead man lay. Some of the men followed Ned Bluecorn up to the body.

Jane and Sassy remained with Ben Moon.

"Was it necessary to kill that man?" Jane asked. "He only took a few dollars and a brooch that had little value."

"That's not the point," said Ben Moon, his voice low and even, his stare unflinching.

"What is the point?" she asked.

"You wouldn't understand," he said.

"How can you be sure?"

"Because if you understood," he said, "you wouldn't have asked the question in the first place."

"You killed him out of principle," she said, "because he stole from you."

"I killed him because he was a damn outlaw and didn't deserve better."

"It would have been better if you hadn't," she said.

"Well, he had a choice," said Ben Moon. But she had already reentered the car with Sassy just a few steps behind her.

Nine

They departed the train in Hays. Jane said they'd have to travel south about fifty miles to reach Sarah's home.

The trip had taken a heavy toll on her. She coughed constantly and was barely able to sit up at all by the time the train stopped in the cow town.

Sassy knew better than anyone how much worse Jane had become, how high a price she had paid for their journey.

"Miss Jane's sick," she said to Ben Moon, preferring to speak to him rather than Ned Bluecorn, whom she feared worse than nightmares.

". . . sicker than she's ever been," sighed Sassy, the whites of her eyes rolling over in her brown face.

Everyone could see it was true.

They took rooms at the Hays House, a square, brick, two-story structure that boasted "20 Clean Rooms & Bath." Jane and Sassy took one room. Ben Moon and Ned took an adjoining one.

As soon as they dropped their bags, Ned volunteered to find a doctor. Sassy insisted she have some privacy in order to bathe and care for Jane. Ben Moon left the hotel and sought the nearest saloon.

McNutts Dance Hall was located south of the tracks, along with the crib houses, gambling dens, and whiskey tents. South of the tracks was where the cowboys went for fun when they brought the cattle in from the long drives up from Texas.

It was the middle of the day and business was slow, which suited Ben Moon just fine.

"New in town?" asked the bartender, a slender man with freckled hands.

"I just arrived. I'll have a whiskey."

The man smiled slightly as he poured the liquor.

Ben Moon drank it down, then set the glass on the polished mahogany bar and indicated the man should pour another.

A few men were playing cards against one wall below a window that needed washing. The light bent yellow through the dusty panes of glass.

"I've seen you somewhere before," said the man behind the bar.

"No. I don't suspect you have," said Ben Moon.

"Yes," said the man, waggling a finger in the air. "Yes, I've seen you. I'm just trying to remember."

Ben Moon had hoped to avoid being recognized. The last thing he desired was to draw attention to himself.

"How much for the bottle?" asked Ben Moon.

"Two dollars."

He paid the man and took the bottle and the glass to a far corner of the room.

He hadn't been there long when he was approached by a man who had been lounging near the card players.

The man had a bloated face marbled with a thousand tiny broken veins in his cheeks and nose. He possessed the sour smell of the unwashed.

"Mind if I join you for a drink, mister?" asked the man.

"I'm not looking for company," said Ben Moon.

The man eyed the bottle and wiped at his mouth with a dark kerchief.

"Maybe you would if you knew who I was," said the man.

"It's not likely, friend."

"Have you ever heard of Wild Bill Hickok?" asked the man. His eyes were rheumy, and his hands shook a great deal.

"I've heard of him."

"Heard of him! Heard of him! Har, ain't that a laugh. Wild Bill was about the most famous man in Kansas!"

"What's your point?"

"Point is," said the man, now in a conspiratorial whisper while at the same time sliding from his pocket a rusted pistol, "I'd be willing to trade you Bill's personal pistol for that bottle of whiskey you're holding onto so dearly."

"How was it you came by Wild Bill's pistol?" Ben Moon questioned, less amused than he appeared.

"Well, now, Bill gave it to me himself. We was lawmen together here in Hays. I saved his damned life once, and he gave me his pistol out of gratitude. That was before the poor bugger went and got himself killed up in the Black Hills."

It was a sad and pitiful ruse.

Ben Moon poured himself a glass of the whiskey and handed over the bottle to the man.

"I'll give you this if you'll leave me my privacy," he said.

The man's face pressed into a rubbery grin, and fluid leaked from the corners of his eyes.

"I hate to give her up, I do," he said, laying the pistol upon the table and taking hold of the bottle. "But, you can't drink iron, now can you?"

It was an old Peacemaker with one of the grips missing and the front sight filed off. It wasn't worth ten cents.

"You were a fool to give ol' Clarence your whiskey for that," said a voice. Ben Moon looked up. It was a woman. It was plain to see she was a working girl.

"Yeah, well it's not every day I get a chance to own Wild Bill's pistol," he said.

"Buy me a drink," she said.

"This sure is a town full of thirsty people," he observed and ordered more whiskey.

She was fairly pretty and at least half his age, maybe even younger. Her eyes were green and gray mixed, and her hair dark but not black. She had a turned-up nose and a heart-shaped mouth. She could have been Jane twenty years back. Except for the turned-up nose.

"You can't be a cowboy," she said. "You're too old."

He laughed.

"We could go to my room—it's in the back—and spend some time together," she offered and then downed the whiskey. She had a way of smiling that pleased him.

"You're bold," he said.

She tossed her head so that the ringlets of her hair bounced.

"A girl like me can't afford to be shy," she replied.

"What's your name?"

"Johanna Lee," she said.

"It's a pretty name." His saying so seemed to please her.

"Come on," she said. "Let's go back to my room."

"No," he said, and she pretended to pout.

"You don't like me," she said. "You don't think I'm pretty."

"Pretty enough for any man," he told her. "I'm just not inclined right now."

"Well, what are you inclined for?" she asked.

"Privacy," he told her.

"You ain't odd are you?"

"How do you mean?"

"I mean you do like women? You're not odd in that way?"

Again he laughed.

"I like 'em well enough."

"Buy me another drink. At least that," she said. "Toby—he's the owner—he won't allow me to sit with a fellow without he at least buys drinks."

"Sure," he said and poured her another glass from the new bottle.

He listened while she talked about life in the frontier town—how lonely it could be when the Texas cowboys weren't in town, how some of the girls she worked with had committed suicide, and how others had married rich men and had become respectable.

It struck him that she would be about the age of Jane's daughter, not much older.

"Most of the girls don't use their real names," she told him. "They're too ashamed. But not me."

She talked like that for well over an hour, and he listened, enjoying the sound of her voice.

"It's a good thing business is slow, mister, or Toby'd have a conniption—me spending all this time with one fellow and just for drinks."

"I guess so," said Ben Moon as he stood and straightened his hat so that it sat comfortably on his head.

"Are you leaving already?" she asked.

"I have business," he said. She looked disappointed, but not too much so. Her eyes searched the room for other

prospects; there were only the men playing cards, the drunk
that had sold him the broken pistol, and the bartender.

"Will you return?" she asked.

"Maybe later," he said.

"I could see to it to only charge you half if you was to
come back later," she said. "Business is mighty slow, and
half a loaf is better'n none." Again she smiled, and again
he felt warmed by it.

He walked down the street, feeling young again because
of her.

He remembered Hays. He had been here before. It had
changed some, but not all that much—more buildings made
of brick; more merchants; more immigrants looking for the
promised land.

The town seemed lonely, though, without the cowboys,
without the great herds of beeves kicking up dust and stink-
ing to high heaven. There was nothing like Texas cowboys
to liven up a town.

Ned Bluecorn ambled down the street, his long arms
swinging as in time with his gait. Several women stepped
aside to allow him to pass, one even stepped out into the
street and then stared after him.

The dark scowl on his face eased up somewhat when he
spotted Ben Moon.

"Jane's taken a turn for the worse," he said.

Ben Moon looked past the Blackfoot toward the Hays
House.

"The doctor's up there with her now. He said the travel
and strain have given her pneumonia and that if the consumption don't kill her, the pneumonia might."

Jane was lying with her eyes closed when Ben and Ned
entered the room. Sassy sat near her bed.

"Miss Jane is sleeping," she said. "Poor thing is wore

out and nearly dead. I've seen sick kittens better off than she is right now."

"The doctor gave her some sort of syrup," said Ned Bluecorn. "It was pink."

"He said it would make her sleep," said Sassy. "He said she needed sleep and rest worse than anything and that she was foolish to travel so far in her condition."

"She don't look too good," said Ned. "She looks like she doesn't have any blood left in her—like she's coughed it all out in those little hankies she carries."

Thirty-five, thirty-six. How old was she? wondered Ben Moon. He didn't know for sure. *It's hard seeing you die like this, Jane. Goddamn but it's hard.*

Ten

"You go on without me, Ben," Jane said when the fever left her. It had taken nearly a week, but she had survived the onset of the pneumonia and had actually seemed better than before.

She sat up in bed and sipped hot tea laced with honey. There was even some color in her cheeks.

"You've come this far," said Ben Moon.

"I know how far I've come," she told him. "Every mile has been torture, more than I could have imagined. I want to see Sarah again. I won't if I go any farther; the journey will see me dead before we reach her."

She seemed brave, far braver than he imagined he himself would be under the circumstances. There were easier ways of dying than slowly.

"I'll go if he won't," said Ned Bluecorn, who stood at the foot of her bed. He rested both hands on the brass footboard. It pained her to see the devotion in his grim, dark features.

"No need," said Ben Moon. "I've already agreed to this job."

"Let Ned go with you, Ben." It was the least she could give him, to let him go along, to be a part of it.

Ned Bluecorn shifted his weight, satisfied by her consideration. Sassy was most pleased with Jane's decision to send both men off.

"I don't mind saying it," Sassy whispered after the two men had left. "But ol' Ned Bluecorn and that Mr. Moon are men marked by sin and trouble. I'd just as soon run into the devil riding a black horse as to run up on either one of them!"

"You are a silly girl," sighed Jane.

"Maybe so, but those men give me the spooks."

They rented saddle horses and asked directions to Claversville, the nearest settlement to the Schultzman homestead. The Schultzmans were Sarah's adoptive parents.

"Due south until you reach the fork, then take the left road," said the liveryman as he saddled their horses—a sandy dun and a tall roan.

"Follow it another twenty-five miles. You have to cross the Willow River. It'll be high this time of year, but there's a ferryman to take you over." The man seemed pleased for the business and for the chance to talk. He seemed to enjoy giving information.

They rode in silence, the sun warming their backs, the gait of the horses easy, comforting.

Several miles out, they came to the fork in the road and veered left.

The land spawned nothing, endless and flat brown all the way to the faded blue horizon.

"They'd be hard pressed to hang a man in this country," said Ben Moon after considering the barren landscape for a time.

"I guess so," said Ned Bluecorn, looking about him for the first time for his thoughts had been on Jane the whole way.

"You ever seen a man hanged, Ned?"

The question was unexpected. The Indian blinked twice, thought about it, concluded he hadn't.

"No."

"I have. It's not a thing that'll leave you, seeing a man hanged."

"I reckon you've seen lots of ugly things," said Ned Bluecorn. "I reckon leading the sort of life you have has caused you to seen plenty of unpleasant things."

"Death comes in lots of ways, but none worse than hanging," said Ben Moon shaking his head slightly as he dropped the knotted reins over the horn of his saddle and reached inside his pocket for his makings.

"I guess next time there's a hanging in the vicinity I'll have to go and see for myself," said Ned Bluecorn, a slight twinge of sarcasm in his voice. All the talk about death troubled him because of Jane's condition.

"Why'd you agree to do this thing for Jane?" he asked.

Ben Moon licked his cigarette and placed one end of it in his mouth. Scraping his thumbnail over a match head, he lighted the cigarette and smoked for a moment.

"She's a friend," he said at last.

"That's all? It ain't because you still love her?"

Ben Moon knew well enough what this line of questioning was leading up to. Ol' Ned was as jealous as a tom cat.

"Oh, I like her." He smiled through a haze of the cigarette smoke. "It's hard not to like Jane. But, I wouldn't consider myself in love with her."

"You was once."

"Well, that's what you keep telling me, Ned."

Ned Bluecorn cleared his throat, spat off to one side, and stared straight ahead. Nothing galled him more than the thought of Ben Moon and Jane together.

They reached the river in the late afternoon. It ran high and muddy brown. They could close their eyes and hear it.

A ferryman watched their approach.

"How do," he said, an expectant look on his face.

Ben Moon nodded; Ned Bluecorn simply stared.

"How much to carry us over?" asked Ben Moon.

"Dollar each."

"High price just to cross a river."

"Well, it's cheaper than drowning," said the ferryman, his mouth splitting open in a gaping grin that displayed stained teeth.

They led their mounts up onto the ferry. The dun was skittish about it, but Ben Moon coaxed him anyway.

"How far yet to Claversville?" asked Ben Moon once they reached the far side of the river.

"A hard ride will get you there by nightfall."

They chose instead to sleep out on the prairie rather than push the rented mounts hard. Miraculously, they found a small copse of cottonwood trees and made camp among them.

"First damn trees I've seen since Montana," said Ben Moon, lifting the saddle from the dun.

"I guess this is where they must come to do their hanging," said Ned Bluecorn wryly.

"I reckon they must," said Ben Moon.

They slept soundly. They never even heard the men approach.

Ned Bluecorn felt something hitting him in the foot. So did Ben Moon.

They opened their eyes and looked up the long barrels of rifles pointing down at them. Men with pink faces and denim coveralls were holding the rifles. Some wore hats. They looked like farmers on a pigeon hunt.

"What are you doing here on this land?" one of the men asked. He was a cock-eyed fellow with flabby jaws and hands so thick his knuckles didn't show. He spoke slowly, deliberately, as though each word were an effort to get out.

"Sleeping," Ben Moon said. "We were sleeping."

"Why?" said the man.

"Because we were tired."

"You ain't from around here," said the man.

"Is that a question?"

"We've had trouble with rustlers," said the man. "Cattle thieves."

"I know what rustlers are," said Ben Moon.

The man eyed the pistols he and Ned Bluecorn wore. "Take those pistols," he ordered another man, a tall skinny fellow wearing a straw hat.

"We're not rustlers," said Ben Moon.

"No way of knowing for certain," said the man. "He looks like *he* could be," he said, nodding toward Ned Bluecorn.

"I'm no goddamn cattle thief!" said Ned.

"You both could be," said the man while the skinny fellow took their pistols. "We've had lots of cattle come up missing lately. A man has to protect his property; you understand that, don't you?"

He could see it in all their faces, the way their eyes flickered with uncertainty—they were scared as hell. Scared that they might shoot somebody or, worse still, get shot themselves. Their own fear made them dangerous.

"I can see where you might take us as trouble," said Ben Moon. "Being strangers and all and sleeping out here on the prairie and you having missing cows. It all seems to add up. But me and that fellow are just passing through, trying to make Claversville. It got late, so we stopped. That's the whole story."

"You look dishonest," said the skinny fellow who had taken their pistols. He had them stuck in his belt. Guns made some men braver than they were.

"Well, you can't hang a man for his looks," said Ben Moon, offering the grin of a possum, "or else me and ol' Ned there would have been dancing with the devil a long time ago."

His lightheartedness seemed to take some of the starch out of their necks. His concern was Ned. The Indian's face was as dark as a summer storm. It didn't take much for a white man to rile Ned's guts. Ned didn't use good judgment when he was mad.

"You see any goddamn cattle around here?" demanded Ned. "Does it look like we stole your goddamn cows?" The questions were heavy with threats and a couple of the pink-faced men pointing their rifles at the Indian took a step backward.

"You're trespassing," said the man with the cock-eye.

"Well, hell, we hadn't meant to," said Ben Moon.

Then, for a time, the men with the pink faces traded looks with one another, unsure of what to do.

They had come upon trespassers, men that could be cattle thieves, men that looked ornery and shiftless. But they had found no stolen cattle—just two men sleeping upon the ground. If they pursued their line of reasoning, there could be gunplay. Someone might get shot or killed. One of these men might have a hideout on him, might pull it, might kill somebody. What would be the point of dying if the strangers hadn't stolen any cattle?

They all knew what the consequences could be; they could feel it down to their bones.

Finally, the man with the cock-eye spoke.

"We don't care who you are, where you're from, or where you are going. All I know is that you are not wanted around here. Saddle your horses and leave before there is real trouble."

The rest was silence. They moved in silence; they saddled their horses in silence; they took back their pistols in silence. And they rode off in silence.

Ned Bluecorn was as mad as hell. Ben Moon was just pleased that he had not been shot by men with pink faces.

They rode a long time in silence away from their camp among the cottonwoods.

"We should've killed those shitheads!" said Ned Bluecorn after several miles.

"What for?" asked Ben Moon, rolling a cigarette between his fingers.

"For pulling guns on us, for kicking us in the feet."

"They were just protecting their property." He thumbed a match into fire and lighted the cigarette.

"We should've killed them anyway," insisted Ned.

"There's no need to kill a man over kicking you in the feet, Ned. Even if it is an insult."

They rode along in more silence.

"Something troubles me about you," said Ned, his voice raspy with pent-up anger.

"I'm not surprised," said Ben Moon.

"You are damn hard to figure out! One man pulls a gun on you and you shoot him in the back. Another does the same and you just ride away. Don't you have any pride at all?"

"That fellow I shot from the train deserved it. Those farmers were just standing their ground, protecting what was theirs. There's a big difference Ned."

"Not to me there ain't. A man sticks a gun in your face—it's all the same in my book."

"Leave it be, Ned."

"Can't."

"Then I guess you'll just have to suffer with it."

"Next man pulls a gun on me, I'm killing! I don't give a damn what his reason."

"It's up to you, Ned," said Ben Moon.

"It's not idle talk," said Ned, challenging.

"No, sir, I didn't suspect it was."

"Damn all white men to hell," said Ned. "Damn you to hell, Ben Moon!"

"Damn me to hell," said Ben Moon.

They rode the rest of the way to Claversville in utter silence, their tongues heavy in their mouths.

Eleven

The boy came in drunk. Stumbling drunk. It was well into night, and the commotion stirred Sam Pepper and the woman, Emma Jordan, from their sleep.

"It's Jesse," she said, sitting up. A shank of moonlight split the room, lay upon the bed, upon the woman. She looked ghostly in the light.

Sam Pepper's only mood was that of irritation at having been awakened at such a late hour.

They could hear the boy swearing, cussing at something he had kicked over in the hallway, a chair, possibly—that spindle-back chair with the red-velvet seat. She had called it an heirloom—her grandparents' parlor chair.

"Can't you go and shut him up?" asked Sam Pepper.

He watched her pull on a chemise, saw how it clung to her shoulders and breasts and hips. His head ached from the port wine they had drunk earlier.

"He gets wild when he drinks," she said, tying the top of the chemise together with its ribbons.

"He ain't but a kid," said Sam Pepper.

"His father left when he was a baby, and I've not taken strong hand with him."

Another crash outside their door, another curse.

"Maybe you should start now," he told her.

He could hear them arguing in the hallway, then farther

down, back toward the kitchen. She was telling him to go to bed; he was telling her to go to hell. It went on like that for several minutes.

Sam Pepper appeared in his underdrawers, a pistol in his right hand.

"Goddamn you, boy; you are disturbing my rest!"

The kid's face was flushed with anger, was gorged with liquored blood.

"You are a son of a bitch!" he said.

"No!" she yelled.

"You are buying trouble," said Sam Pepper, raising the gun to shoulder level.

She stepped between them. Her hair hung in limp strands; her eyes were wide and fearful.

"Please—" she begged.

He had already cocked the pistol. He felt the initial pressure of his finger on the trigger.

The boy seemed shaken; the color was gone from his face. The man meant to kill him. The realization was sobering. He started to speak, to protest his murder, but found it impossible to do so. The fear was like a rope that strangled him.

The three of them stood there, not moving, for a long, full moment.

"I am no son of a bitch!" said Sam Pepper without lowering the pistol.

The boy stammered, muttered something unintelligible.

"What did you say?" demanded the gunman.

"I . . . I said, no sir, you ain't no son of a bitch."

Jesse Jordan could see the wormy veins between the man's flesh and skull; could see, too, the poisonous eyes and thin grim mouth. What made him think he could come home and challenge such a man? A man who was all bone and knotted skin and darkness.

His drunkenness fled him, taking with it his angry bravado.

"I should kill you for the practice," said Sam Pepper.

Jesse Jordan tasted bile in his throat.

"Let him go to bed, Mr. Pepper. Please!" Her voice was thin and breaking as though she were about to cry. It was late; he was tired and had a headache. He eased the hammer of the pistol down.

"You should learn some manners," he said. "Maybe you ought to take your blanket and sleep outdoors tonight so's not to disturb me further." It was a command, not a suggestion.

He returned to her room and sat on the edge of the bed, his nerves raw. Several minutes later, Emma Jordan entered her bedroom and found him there.

"What gives you the right to come into my house and threaten my son?" she demanded.

He turned slowly to face her.

"I'll not take cursing from anybody," he said.

"He's just a boy! Not even sixteen years old, and you were going to murder him over a curse!"

"It doesn't matter to me, his age. If he's old enough to insult, he's old enough to suffer the consequences."

"I want you to leave my house!"

"Not tonight, sister. I'm wore out."

"You will leave," she said.

"If I don't?"

"I will go and get the constable and have you removed."

"I think not," he said, a slow, dry smile pressing his lips.

"Are you threatening me as well?"

"No."

"Then what is to stop me?"

"Maybe you don't know who I am, Mrs. Jordan. But I can damn well guarantee that whatever law you have here will have heard of me. I don't think any man is willing to put his life in jeopardy over a squabble about where I spend the night."

"You think big of yourself," she said, her skin feeling hot with anger and frustration.

"Well, I have a right," he said. "I have killed enough men and have earned the right to think big of myself. Now come to bed!"

She was stunned by the suggestion. What earlier had attracted her, now appalled her. He seemed the devil incarnate.

"I cannot," she protested.

"Yes," he said. "Yes, you will."

Later, she lay in the dark, the moonlight gone from the room, and listened to the slow steady rhythm of his breathing.

Afraid to move, she lay motionless in the darkness, the bitter taste of tears in her mouth. Her anguish was that of shame. Shame not for herself, but for that suffered by her son Jesse at the hands of the man lying next to her.

She had been a fool. A lonely fool, and now it had nearly cost her her son's life.

Morning found him shaving, his galluses down, dressed all but for a shirt. He drew the thin sharp blade of the straight razor across the taut skin of his cheeks and chin, scraping thick soapy lather and beard in slow sure motions.

He looked at her in the small mirror he had mounted above the sink in the kitchen. He let his gaze linger on her for a brief time, then returned his attention to his shaving.

She busied herself with the preparation of a meager breakfast: Coffee, leftover biscuits, fried pork.

She had gone first to Jesse's room, but he had not been there. She looked for him outside and found him sleeping on the ground, a blanket wrapped around him.

"Get up," she said, touching his shoulder. He opened his eyes slowly. It looked as though he might have been crying; his eyes were red and swollen.

"Get up and come in for breakfast," she said.

"No," he told her.

"Because of him?"

The boy nodded. He seemed barely a child.

"Don't worry about him," she said. "He promised that he would be leaving the first thing. Come inside."

Sam Pepper finished his shave, examined his face with the tips of his fingers, searching for rough spots, spots he had missed. There were none. Satisfied, he wiped his face with a towel and sat down at the table.

She poured him coffee and set the biscuits and fried pork before him.

Jesse sat at the far end, his eyes lowered.

Sam Pepper ate without comment. He chewed his food without any indication of its taste. He drank his coffee; he did not sip it. When he had finished, he stared at the two of them—the woman and the boy.

"I could have killed you last night, you know," he said, his attention on Jesse Jordan. "I could have killed you and not lost a minute's worth of sleep."

The boy's stomach knotted.

"You remember that, kid. You remember how close you came to buying it from Sam Pepper. You remember, too, that I let you live. You remember and be grateful for it."

He then turned his attention to the woman.

"You remember it, too."

She could taste only her hatred for him. Then, he did an odd thing: He kissed her on the forehead, a light delicate kiss that felt like the wings of a butterfly.

They watched from a window, partially pulling back one of the curtains, discreetly observing him as he walked down the middle of the street, his Winchester cradled in the crook of one arm. And at last, she allowed herself to breathe.

"He is nothing at all like the stories I've read about him," said Jesse.

"No, I suppose he isn't," she agreed.

"The stories made me believe he was heroic."

"They are just books," she said. "They don't know."

"He's nothing but a son of a bitch!" said Jesse. The epithet caused her to look at him, her face a mask of sadness. "Well, that is all that he is, a son of a bitch!"

She wasn't so sure.

Twelve

The doctor came each morning. He was a thin-faced man with bony wrists and hands and long spidery fingers. He smelled faintly of pipe tobacco; and when he spoke to her, his front teeth revealed themselves. They were like the teeth of a rodent, curved and yellow and long.

He would first place one of his smooth cool hands upon her forehead. Then, he would bend and press his ear to her chest and listen to her breathing, to her heart. She could see his shiny hard scalp through the sparseness of his silver hair.

Finally, he would examine one of the stained hankies.

His routine was always the same.

"You are a very lucky woman to have survived the pneumonia," he told her.

"Only to die of lung fever," she said.

"Yes . . . I suppose so," he admitted, acknowledging openly her cynicism at his inability to heal her. The lines in his long face deepened, his gaze drifted from her pale features to the blue-flocked wallpaper of the room.

"I'm sorry," she said. "I didn't mean to sound ungrateful for your efforts."

He raised a bony hand, touched the air with it. "I understand your frustration," he said. "I would most likely feel the same given your condition."

"How long?" she asked. "How long do I have to live?"

He rubbed the knobby chin of his face with his rawboned fingers. He had the eyes of an old hound.

"It would only be a guess," he said.

"How long?"

"A few weeks. Possibly a month, maybe two. Your lungs. . . . They're not good. The pneumonia didn't help any."

"There is nothing to be done?"

"No."

She turned her attention to Sassy, who sat opposite the doctor.

"Sassy, I'd like you to go and get me some whiskey."

"But, Miss Jane, you don't drink whiskey," the girl corrected.

"Do as I say, child. Don't be quarrelsome."

Sassy looked exasperated at the request. She implored the doctor with a wide-eyed stare. His own eyes seemed to smile perceptively.

"It'll mean going to town. I'll have to put on my shoes and go to town, Miss Jane."

"Then please do so, and don't be the entire day."

"Yes'm."

Jane returned her attention to the doctor.

"How much do I owe you for your services?"

He shrugged his shoulders beneath the black broadcloth coat he wore, a coat that was frayed at both collar and cuffs.

"Ten dollars should cover everything," he said tentatively. "I can keep coming each morning if you like," he added. "I can help see you through."

"It's a kind offer," she replied, reaching inside a small, black-velvet handbag studded with pearls. "But, I don't require that anyone watch me die. That is all that you'd be doing, is it not?"

He took the money she handed him and studied it for a moment before putting it in his coat pocket.

Nodding, he said, "I'm afraid that is true."

"Then there is no need." His walk was not as much a walk as a shuffle; and when he left the room, he did not bother to say more or to look back.

There was a quietude in the room once he had left. She could hear the soft thumping of her heart, the labors of her breathing.

She would not cry, she promised herself. She would not cry in self-pity or out of fear. But she was bitter about dying too soon. And when she thought about Sarah, about possibly not being able to see the girl in time, she gave in to her tears. Sassy found her with wet stains upon her cheeks.

"Lordy, Miss Jane." But what to do? Jane had been good to her all these years. She had treated her like kin—not quite like a daughter, but close enough—so that she had developed a strong fondness toward her mistress.

It pained her to see Jane crying soft, choked sobs. A woman cries like that, she's hurt deep. Sassy had seen her mother after the white men put a rope around her daddy's neck and strung him from a tree stained black from the rain.

She had been too young to know why they had hanged her daddy. And at first her mama had cried loud and hollered and pulled at her clothes. But later, after her daddy had been laid in the ground, her mama spent her days crying soft and silent tears. Like Jane.

Her mama had told her it was the kind of hurt you couldn't get rid of.

"I brung your whiskey, Miss Jane," she said, holding the bottle of amber liquid aloft.

Without bothering to fist away her tears, she said, "Pour us each a glass, Sassy."

"Oh no, Miss Jane. I never have drunk the stuff in my life!"

"It's time you did, then."

Sassy had heard Ned Bluecorn talk about the evils of drink, about how it had killed some of the men in his family. She had witnessed many a man drunk or nearly so in the big house back in the days when it had been alive and full of fun. She dreaded the thought of tasting the stuff. But pour she did.

She would not be a further disappointment to Jane. If it was what Jane wanted her to do, then she surely would. It stung as if she had a mouth full of bees. The taste was awful.

"Give it a chance," said Jane, enjoying for the first time in a long while the burn of good hard liquor.

The second swallow wasn't as bad, but still horrible. The third came more easily. By the time she had drained that glassful, she didn't mind that Jane told her to pour them each another.

They drank the golden whiskey and watched the yellow sun from their window. Sassy swore she had never seen the light so beautiful, and Jane agreed.

"Will you be sorry to die, Miss Jane?" she asked as innocently as a child. Her head was dull, numb as if it were stuffed with cotton; her tongue had grown fat and heavy.

"I will," said Jane. "There was a time in my life when it would not have mattered to me, a time when I might have even welcomed it. Being a whore was not easy."

Jane's words struck Sassy as funny and she giggled, spilling whiskey onto the counterpane.

"You are a curious child," said Jane, a whimsical smile

upon her lips. The whiskey was working its magic—on both of them.

"Oh, Miss Jane, what's it like to be a whore?" Sassy's teeth were as white as pearls; her eyes glittered; she was as drunk as a possum.

"I have corrupted you, child," laughed Jane. Her sadness seemed now distant, buried deep within her bones.

"Oh, Miss Jane. If only we had us some men here, we'd have a party—just like before you got down sick."

"Yes. Yes," cried Jane clapping her hands in delight.

"We'd have ol' Tink playin' on the piano and get the men to dance with us! Just like before!"

Their heads filled with memories; their ears could hear the music and the laughter. They saw the happy faces.

"You was so elegant in your pretty dresses, Miss Jane. Especially the green satin one," said Sassy, wistfully.

"When I die, you can have all my dresses," said Jane.

"Do you mean it?" Sassy's eyes grew wide and round with the news.

"Of course."

"But what about Miss Erma and Miss Minnie and Miss Marie?"

"I have made arrangements, a portion for each. You are all included."

"You were always good to us girls, Miss Jane. Now you are leaving us on our own. We will be forever lonely without you." Sassy's mood had grown suddenly maudlin and she wept.

"You are overcome from the alcohol," said Jane, her own spirits undampened. It seemed better to talk about it than to keep it inside, the dying.

Sassy's thin brown shoulders heaved up and down. She

sprawled on the floor below the window and its slanting light and bawled uncontrollably.

"You are making me sad," said Jane. "If you do not stop, I will ask you to leave the room."

Sassy tried to speak, but her crying seemed a flood that swept away all words.

Jane poured herself another glass of whiskey and sipped it. The girl cried on, and the woman's thoughts turned to Ben Moon.

What would it have been like if she and Ben had married years ago? she asked herself. Would she have been different? Would he?

The whiskey had begun its work in earnest. She felt the heaviness of her eyelids, arms, and legs. She had gotten good and drunk, exactly what she had wanted.

She didn't care anymore about dying, or living. She didn't care anymore about Ben Moon and what might have been. She felt only the peaceful invasion of the alcohol coursing through her veins, shutting down the senses on its journey.

Sassy cried.

Jane thought about Sarah.

And the sun eased downward beyond the flat plain of prairie, sending a final burst of golden rays into the gathering clouds.

Thirteen

It rained. Hard silver rain that pelted them. Rain that knocked down the brims of their hats and soaked their clothes.

They reached Claversville mid-morning and asked directions to the Schultzman homestead, to Karl and Hanna's place, to Jane's baby daughter grown up.

They stood under the awning of a dry goods store and spoke with its proprietor. He was a man with crisp blue eyes and handlebar mustaches and a clean white apron. He had been standing under the awning watching the rain as it danced on the mud-slicked street. He leaned slightly on the handle of a broom, and the rain drummed on the canvas above their heads.

"We are looking for the Schultzman place," Ben Moon said.

The man said, "I'm Jacob Bledsoe, and this is my store." He had a broad face and a smile to match. "You gents should come in and buy yourselves some slickers—this rain is terrible."

"Do you know Karl Schultzman?" Ben tried again. "He has a homestead around here."

"Come, step inside. I have a fire going in the stove," invited Jacob Bledsoe.

They huddled by the fire rubbing their hands while the

man went to a shelf and took down two rubber slickers and laid them on the counter.

"Schultzman," the man repeated, his hands spreading out the slickers. "I'm fairly new to these parts. I am from Iowa. Arrived less than two months ago. Would you care to try these on?"

Ned Bluecorn asked, "How much?"

The man smiled pleasantly. "Five dollars each. A good bargain considering."

"Considering what?" pressed Ben Moon.

"Considering a man could catch his death in a rain such as this."

"We are already wet," said Ned Bluecorn, feeling the heat of the stove reach through his wet clothes and warm his skin.

"I don't know of any Schultzman," said the man, reaching inside a jar of hard candy. Hoarhound. "Would you care for some?" He extended his hand. Ned Bluecorn took two pieces and put them in his mouth.

"Who might?" asked Ben. "Who might know where the Schultzmans live?"

The man thought for a moment, his mouth savoring the sweetness of the hoarhound candy.

"I suppose anybody that's lived here longer than I would probably be able to tell you about those folks," he said. "I'd try Constable Hargrave. His office is just down the street, other side."

Ben Moon laid out ten dollars for the slickers.

Ned Bluecorn looked surprised.

"I don't feel like getting wet anymore," Ben told the Indian.

Constable Hargrave was grizzled and gaunt, as knotted as old hickory. He wore a five-point star pinned to his coat, and when the door rattled open he came to with a start. He

ad been dozing, dreaming of a race horse he had once
owned.

His small eyes were the color of bloody egg yolks.

"Har!" he said, surveying his unexpected visitors. He sat
bolt upright. The pair looked like trouble to him.

"We are looking for Karl Schultzman," said the clear-
eyed, leaner man. His companion was an Indian. The constable didn't care much for Indians.

"Why?" demanded Hargrave, his voice cracked and
phlegmy. "Why do you want to find Karl Schultzman?"

"Personal reasons," Ben Moon answered shortly.

The Indian chewed noncommittally on a plug of tobacco.

"Don't I know you?" asked the lawman, squinting. The
white man looked familiar.

"No," said Ben Moon. "I'd remember."

These were hard cases if he'd ever seen any, and he'd
seen plenty in his day.

"I suggest you keep ridin'. You and your red companion."

The lids of Ned Bluecorn's eyes lifted slowly, exposing
the whiteness of hard-boiled eggs, pupils as black as tar, a
stare as deadly as a viper's.

The old man's craw slipped up and down beneath the
loose skin of his throat; and the corners of his mouth,
streaked and stained by tobacco juices, drew tight.

"We didn't come all this way for chatter or suggestions,
friend," said Ben Moon. "And it would be unpleasant to
have to kill you over a question."

Constable Hargrave found the white man's clear-eyed
gaze even more menacing than that of the Indian. The old
man's back teeth began to ache.

"I don't want no trouble, mister. They don't pay me
enough for real trouble." The effort at grinning off the threat
of the two men failed.

Ned Bluecorn parted his coat and showed the butt of his pistol.

"The old Dutchman died a few months back," said the constable.

"Schultzman?"

"Yeah. Cholera!"

"His woman?"

"Her, too."

"They had a girl, a daughter, near eighteen."

"She's gone."

"Where?"

"I don't know. She didn't say; I didn't ask. She stayed around awhile after the old folks died. She stayed up in that house all alone and kept to herself. Then one day, we saw her ride out."

"Alone?"

"No. She rode out with a gambler who had drifted in a few weeks before. A man named Pierce. I think I heard him called Doc. He's rumored to have a reputation."

The name struck a chord. Ben Moon had known a Doc Pierce back in Indian Territory before the land rush.

The old lawman seemed satisfied with himself, pleased that he hadn't asked for trouble or gotten any.

"Which way were they headed?" asked Ben Moon.

"They took the road to Dodge. They were riding in the Dutchman's buggy, a fancy cab pulled by a gray. Pierce had his piebald tied on back."

Ben Moon turned toward the door. Ned Bluecorn threw one last hard look at the constable then followed suit.

"Say, I remember you now," the old man called out. "You're Ben Moon. I seen you kill a man over in Wichita. A cowboy."

They stepped out into the street, into the rain that wasn't
s bad now that they were wearing the new rubber slickers.

"What now?" asked Ned Bluecorn.

"I guess we go to Dodge."

"What makes you think they'll stop in Dodge?"

"Because Dodge City is about the goddamnedest place
n the plains. And if that fellow Sarah is with is the same
Doc Pierce I know, he'll surely find Dodge to his liking."

"How far do you figure?" said Ned Bluecorn. "My guts
re aggravating me; I could eat this horse."

They reached Dodge an hour after dark. The rain had
slackened, turning to mist.

Dodge was a town sprouted from the prairie grass: Tents
nd raw lumber buildings, dance halls and whiskey dens.
And a railroad. It was a town that had grown up fast and
ard, fed by the wages of Texas cowboys, watered by their
lood.

But it was spring and not as rowdy as it would be later
vhen the trail herds came in, the trail herds and the wild
owboys that drove them.

He remembered those boys all too well. Wide-eyed and
outhful; kids with big appetites and big pistols. Some of
hem not old enough to grow whiskers, but old enough to
rive a cow a thousand miles and eat dust for three months
f the year.

He remembered.

They liked to drink and they liked to raise hell, and some-
imes they did too much of both. Three months broke and
ne day rich. It proved too much for most of them. The
vhores and the whiskey and the gamblers picked them as
lean as stewing chickens.

He remembered.

He wore a frock coat and a string tie and a black som-

brero. He carried a Hamilton double-barreled shotgun or
rounds and a pistol in each pocket. He went well-armed for
trouble could be had at any turn, in any dance hall or whiskey parlor.

Texas cowboys!

He remembered.

"Who is this Doc Pierce?" asked Ned Bluecorn as they
approached the town from the north. Squares of greasy yellow light shone from the windows of the buildings.

"He's a professional gambler, a fancy dresser. He has
killed a few men."

"What would Jane's girl be doing with someone like
that?"

"Doc's got a reputation with the ladies. He's been described as handsome. Other than that, I couldn't say."

They reined in at Dog Kelly's place, a false-fronted saloon. Ben Moon remembered it as having a fine oak bar
with lots of mirrors.

There was a keno game going on in one corner of the
long room. Overhead, a stamped tin ceiling reflected golden
light from the hanging whale-oil lights. The long bar was
still there; so were the mirrors.

Kelly had added a large painting of a Rubenesque woman
with flowing hair reclining on a divan. The woman was
wrapped in sheer red scarfs.

Ned Bluecorn stared at the woman a long time. Ben
Moon ordered whiskey.

"There's not much left for a man to wonder about," said
the Indian staring up at the picture. "She's practically naked."

"That's probably why Kelly put her up there," said Ben
Moon, a thin smile of amusement creasing the old growth
of beard around his mouth.

"A man could do all right with a woman like that," Ned Bluecorn observed absently.

"As long as she didn't fall on him," said Ben Moon.

Ned Bluecorn allowed his gaze to drift from the painting to the passive countenance of Ben Moon.

"You're having fun with me."

"No, Ned. Just stating a fact."

The dark face of Ned Bluecorn expressed uncertainty. Was he being fooled with? He wondered how the aging gunfighter would stand up in a fistfight. It was something that he himself had learned to do early in life, fight with his hands—and feet. He had gotten good enough at it to have done some prizefighting for a white man in Red Lodge.

Hitting men with his fists, knocking them down and down again until they could no longer stand, was something he had grown to enjoy. There was a pleasure in the power of it that he had not known otherwise. Even taking the blows of other men as they fought back aroused him. The salty taste of his own blood did not offend.

It had been a long time since he had last fought. He wondered about it like some men might wonder about a woman they had once known and loved.

"Don't have fun with me," he said.

"It's not our time yet, Ned," said Ben Moon, ordering a second glass of whiskey.

"You make sure and let me know when," said the Blackfoot.

"Yeah, I'll make sure you get an invitation."

Ben Moon surveyed the room, the faces, looking for that of Doc Pierce. He remembered him as small, not more than five-six or seven. He had an angular face with eyes almost as black as those of Ned Bluecorn's. Back then, Doc Pierce had sported a thin black mustache and had a peculiar way of holding his head cocked to one side when gambling, as though that were the only way for him to read his cards.

The one other thing he remembered about Doc was that the man always went armed and, like most professional gamblers, was a good shot. Doc was said to have killed several men—seldom over a woman. Always over cards.

Doc wasn't in Dog Kelly's.

"We'll need to find a place to flop for the night."

"It's stopped raining," said Ned Bluecorn. "We could camp outside of town."

"Not me," said Ben Moon. "I've gotten too used to a bed to sleep on the ground."

"You're spending Jane's money awful freely," replied the Indian.

"You don't have to sleep in a bed if you don't want to, Ned. It's your choice."

Ned Bluecorn shrugged his shoulders.

"I guess there's no reason for you to have the pleasure of a bed while I sleep on the ground," he said. "You sleep in a bed, so do I."

"It makes sense," said Ben Moon.

"I could stand some beef and beans," said the Indian. He felt that deep kind of hunger that crawls into the belly and wrenches at the guts like a big hole that needs filling up.

Ben Moon barely noticed. He had grown used to living off whiskey and cigarettes and old memories.

Fourteen

Death had come suddenly. Karl had simply come home from town one afternoon.

"I don't feel so well," he told Hanna.

Hanna, her apple-cheeks glowing red from the heat of the cook stove that she and Sarah stood over baking strudels, looked at her husband. His flesh was the color of flour.

"What is wrong with you, Karl?"

"I don't know," he said. "This morning, I was okay. I only went to town to get you these apples and to visit with some of the men. Then, the next thing I know, I am feeling sick to myself."

"*Ya,* you look like you are not so good," Hanna said, wiping her rough, reddened hands on the muslin apron she wore. She went to him and placed a hand on his forehead.

"I stopped at Mr. Yussef's on my way and we talked," said Karl, shaking his head and sitting down on a chair. "I told him I wanted to buy one of his pigs for butchering so that we will have enough meat over the winter."

Sarah tugged at her father's boots and set them by the back door.

"Bring me a glass of schnapps," he asked her. "Maybe I will feel better with some schnapps in my belly."

She could smell the wool of his clothes as she brought him his glass of schnapps. It was a kind, comforting smell.

"I am worried about your father," her mother said later that evening as they sat at the large oak table eating their supper. Karl had taken to his bed shortly after arriving home, and Sarah and Hanna ate alone. The table seemed larger without him there.

"I think he will be all right," Sarah assured her.

"He is getting on in years," Hanna said softly.

"He is strong, Mama."

By late that evening, she could hear her father retching. She drew the bed covers up to her chin and listened to his agony in the far bedroom.

She heard her mother's muffled supplications. "Oh, Karl. Oh, Karl!"

In the morning, he was no better.

"I will go and get the doctor and bring him here to have a look at your father," Hanna said, already putting on her heavy coat and wrapping a scarf around her head. "See if you can get him to drink some soup. I have made a good broth of chicken."

She listened to the sound of the grandfather clock ticking in the hallway after her mother left. The silence of the house was heavy.

His skin was hot to the touch and when he slept, it was in fits and starts.

She changed his bedding several times that day and tried to ignore, as much as possible, the unpleasantness.

She fed him the broth with the white pieces of chicken floating in it. He was unable to keep it down. His vomiting stained the sheets and his nightshirt. His sickness made the room warm and sour, but she stayed with him. And when she could stand the room no longer, she stood in the yard and let the cold December air bite her skin until she could no longer stand that either.

Hanna found the doctor at the Yussefs' home. They were both ill, and Hanna waited patiently in the parlor for him to come from their rooms.

"They are very sick," the doctor told her. "I believe it is the cholera. I believe it is from bad water in their well."

She remembered then that Karl had stopped there the day before. When she returned to her own home with the doctor, they found that Karl had grown delirious with fever.

"I have fields to plow," he said over and over. "The cows have not come home yet." His ramblings made no sense to her. They did not farm. Karl was a shoemaker and a harness maker. They owned no cows.

"I believe he has the cholera," said the doctor. "Like the others."

In two days, Karl was dead. Sarah helped her mother wash his body. He had grown thin in those few days. His ribs showed, and the ridges of his hip bones and the hollows of his cheeks. His feet were long and bony and blanched. He seemed so frail in death.

They buried Karl in the flat brown prairie. Their neighbors used pick axes and shovels to dig a grave, for the earth had grown hard from the winter. Already, Hanna showed the first signs of the sickness.

The Yussefs, Joseph and Ruth, passed away just days later and were buried by the same men neighbors bearing their picks and shovels across their shoulders, their faces grim to the task.

The doctor said there was little he could do.

Hanna went quietly in her sleep, and again the neighbors came. The women helped wash her and dress her in a black dress, and the men tortured the frozen ground with their tools until the ground gave in and accepted her.

Sarah waited for her own death. Surely death would come

to her as well. The doctor said that cholera was a terrible affliction that sometimes took whole communities. Four already in their small band of neighbors.

She waited, prepared for the sickness that would cause her to vomit and foul her bedding and drain the life from her, just the way it had from her beloved Karl and Hanna.

She held their heavy Bible in her lap, but did not read it.

She was embarrassed that she did not weep; not once did tears come to her eyes. She remembered Hanna's telling her that those who do not cry on sad occasions are often with the greatest sorrow. She hoped that that was true.

The ensuing days passed slowly, the winter light dull and gray, the darkness coming early in the evening. Often she sat in the dark and thought about them.

No one came to see her. Not one neighbor. She realized after a time that they were afraid. They feared the cholera that waited in the house with her.

"I am not afraid of you," she said to the walls of the house. "If you are waiting for me, I am here." The clock in the hallway ticked and chimed on the hour as it always had.

The tom cat that had been her mother's pet came for feeding and sometimes rubbed against her legs and meowed to be let out as it always had.

Her sleep, and ultimately, hunger came, as it always had. But death stayed away.

Then, one morning as she was dressing, she heard a knock at the door.

He was a stranger, a man whose eyes were dark but not somber. He smiled when he removed his hat and bowed slightly.

He said his name was Elihue Pierce but he was often

alled Doc. He wanted to know if he could water his horse
nd rest in the yard. He explained that he had been long
a the saddle and that now his horse limped from the cold,
r perhaps a shard of rock.

"Why?" she had asked.

"Why what, Miss?"

"Why are you called Doc if your name is Elihue?"

His smile broadened.

"Because I used to practice dentistry," he said.

"And do you still?"

He laughed, but not derisively.

"Oh no, Miss. It was a profession I was poorly suited
or, staring into other folks' mouths." He laughed again,
eld up a gloved hand with one finger bent and hidden. "A
ellow could lose his digits."

He was older than she, but not terribly so. Not like most
f the men in Claversville. She judged perhaps ten years
lder.

She invited him in from the cold. He insisted on attending
is animal first. She considered it admirable that he did.

When he finally entered the house, he stamped both feet
nd slapped his hands together, his handsome face ruddy
rom the chill air.

She had boiled water for tea and sliced pieces of a fruit-
ake left over from Christmas. Karl had bought it in town
rom Mrs. Klimmel, and it was as heavy as an anvil.

The man seemed pleased that she was offering him tea
nd fruitcake.

"I have not eaten fruitcake in years." He smiled.

"It may not be very good," she said.

He tasted it and smiled again.

She was glad to see him enjoying it. She sliced more.
Ie washed it down with the tea.

"You are a savior," he said. "A beautiful savior."

She felt her skin flush with embarrassment.

"You are simply hungry. That is plain to see," she told him.

"Yes. Hungry and cold and weary. Two days ago I was caught in a storm north of here. I've experienced many things, but nothing like a snowstorm on the plains. I feel lucky to be alive."

His eyes never left her; when he spoke or ate or drank his tea, his eyes never once left her.

"What are you doing here?" she asked.

"I was on my way to Dodge," he told her. "Have you been to Dodge?"

She shook her head. "Father said it was a sinful place. We never went."

"Your father is right. It is not a place for a woman like you." He looked around. "Do you live here alone?"

"This is my father's house," she told him. "My father and mother died of the cholera one month ago."

His gaze returned to her. "I'm sorry," he said.

It had been so long since she had heard another voice in the house—so terribly, terribly long since she had had a visitor.

He said, "Look." It begun to snow outside.

Whether it was the snow, or his unexpected company, it broke something in her—something that raised itself in her chest and caught itself in her throat—and she began to cry.

"I feel as though I have lost everything," she told him through the tears.

"It's no wonder," he said gently.

"No one comes anymore now that Mama and Papa are dead. I feel as though I cannot go beyond the walls of these

oms." She saw her pain reflected in his eyes, and it filled
er all the more with sorrow.

"I should leave," he said. "I should not be here."

"No. Please stay," she said.

Her feelings became waves washing upon a shore. She
nd her parents had once traveled to San Francisco by train
nd she had stood on a long wooden pier and watched the
cean run itself upon the shoreline, breaking upon the
ocks, retreating, and returning. Everything inside her felt
ke that now: The sorrow, the loneliness, the joy of having
ompany at last.

He stayed for dinner, a meager meal of cooked carrots
nd the last portions of a cured ham brought by neighbors
hen they had buried first Karl and then Hanna.

His eyes never left her.

They spoke awkwardly, intermittently, sampling the food,
rying to find the right words to offer one another. He
eemed patient with her. She liked that.

Afterward, he examined his horse and said that the hoof
eemed split and asked if there were someone local that
night care for the animal. She told him about Mr. McGee,
ne blacksmith who owned the livery.

"Can I come and visit you again?" he asked.

"I thought you were going to Dodge," she said.

"Only when this fellow is ready to ride again," he told
er, stroking the muzzle of the piebald horse. It had light-
olored eyes.

"I don't know how to feel about you, Mr. Pierce."

He hunched his shoulders.

"No need to feel anything, Miss Schultzman. It's just that
thought you could use the company and I know that I
an."

She had consented to his visiting again. And later, long

after he had left for town, she wondered what dark, dar
secrets he held. She was surely attracted to him.

His stay had lasted more than a week. He came to vis
every day, and once it warmed unseasonably and they wer
for a picnic.

"What will you do here now that your folks have passed?"
he asked that pleasant day.

"I don't know."

"It seems you would be wasting your life to stay here."

"Papa was the first to die of the cholera," she said. "I
seems everyone feels he was the cause of the sickness sinc
he was the first one. They seldom speak to me anymore
the others."

"Why stay, then?" he said.

"I don't know."

"You are very pretty," he said.

"And you say nice things to me," she told him. "I wonde
if it is because you know that I am lonely."

"I say nice things to you because they are true."

"What do you do for a living, Elihue?" She was gla
they no longer referred to each other by their last names
She was comfortable with their growing familiarity.

"I won't lie to you," he said. "I am a gambler."

"You can earn your way by being a gambler?"

"When you're as good at it as I am," he said, "you can."

"Are you as good at it as you were at dentistry," she asked

"I like it more."

"Is it dangerous?"

"Not usually. I run a straight game."

"Tell me why you prefer it over what you've been edu
cated to do."

He smiled, pushed back the brim of his hat, and lifted
piece of fried chicken from the picnic basket.

"Well, I reckon what I like best about it is, I get to travel, see the country, to meet all kinds of folks. I like the lventure."

The way he told it made it seem romantic, and his hand-me face took on a boyishness.

"This is good fried chicken, Sarah. The best."

"Would you take me with you when you go to Dodge?"

He stopped working on the drumstick he held and stared her.

"Dodge would only be a stop along the way," he said.

"I understand."

"Do you understand the rest of it?" he asked.

"I understand only that my staying here in this place will ave me forever lonely."

He nodded.

"Well, I guess you understand well enough then. I plan a leaving in the morning."

She felt their stares as they rode through town in Karl's ıggy. But what did it matter now, she told herself. They atched her with simple faces, surprised but not sorry to e her go. She had been a wonderful girl, but the sickness d changed everything.

They thought, *Maybe now we don't have to be afraid ıymore.*

Fifteen

They rose early.

"Where to?" asked Ned Bluecorn.

"I reckon anyone knows about professional gamblers i[n] town," said Ben Moon, "it would be the law."

"I could stand to eat first," said Ned.

"It'll wait."

They found the jail and the city marshal's office all i[n] one building. Several men lounged within. Their star[k] wind-burned faces came to bear upon the two stranger[s]. The loungers all wore badges pinned to their vests, cartridg[e] belts, and pistols. Some were hatless.

One man in particular drew the interest of Ben Moo[n] he was square-built with close-cropped hair.

"Bill," said Ben Moon.

The man did not looked pleased at the recognition.

"What are you doing in Dodge?" he asked. Ned Blueco[rn] noticed he was wearing two pistols. "And who is the I[n] dian?"

"You ain't changed any, Bill. That's easy to see."

"What do you mean by that?"

"Ned, this here is Marshal Billy Tibbs, famous fronti[er] lawman."

Ben Moon said it as if he were trying to get a bad tast[e] out of his mouth. Ned saw how the lawman's jaw muscle[s]

ghtened into knots just below his ears. It was also obvious
at Billy Tibbs did not care for Ben Moon.

"Let it rest, Moon."

"When'd you hit Dodge, Billy?"

"I'd ask the same of you."

"Last I heard, you were working a game up in Leaven-
orth."

"Yeah, well that was a long time ago," growled the law-
an.

"How's the action here, Billy? Are there plenty of faro
ames and whores to run for a man that could see the op-
ortunity?"

"I asked what you're doing in Dodge."

"We came to check on a fellow, a gambler by the name
f Doc Pierce. As I recall, you two know each other."

"Doc's not in town."

"Talk has it he was headed this way."

"I said he's not in town!"

"He's traveling with a young woman," said Ben Moon.
You know Doc and women. He's never without one."

"I'd know if he were here, and he ain't! So clear out
ourself before I run you in for vagrancy."

The stark-faced deputies had the focused stares of trained
atchdogs.

"What was that all about?" asked Ned Bluecorn after
ey had left the lawman's office and stood on the sidewalk.

"Billy Tibbs and I go way back together," said Ben
Moon, rolling a cigarette.

"I had to shoot him once. He's never forgiven me."

"That's it?"

"Well, the trouble was the bullet went through him and
illed his brother."

"I can see why he'd be bothered by that."

"It was his brother I was aiming for when Billy decide to step between us. He always was dumb like that."

They stepped into the street and barely avoided a wago full of raw lumber being pulled by a team of lathere horses. The teamster swore at them. "Get the hell out o the way!"

"I went up there to arrest Billy's brother Ike," continue Ben Moon, displaying a passion for finishing the story now that it had presented itself.

"I was a deputy U.S. Marshal and Ike was suspected o stealing horses from the government. This was back in th Nations. I always suspected Billy had a role in the stealin, as well, but I never could prove it.

" 'Ike,' I say when I get up there. 'I am arresting yo for stealing government horses.' " They had crossed to th far side of the street, and Ben Moon stepped inside a saloon Ned followed.

Ben Moon paused in his story long enough to order whiskey.

"Are you thirsty?" he asked Ned Bluecorn.

"A beer, maybe."

"Now Ike's about as dumb as a chicken," continued Be Moon, tasting his whiskey with a slow deliberateness.

"Ike's not as dumb as Billy, of course. But close. Ik says, 'I ain't stole no government horses, and you can' prove it.' "

Ned Bluecorn sipped his beer slowly and eyed a jar fille with pickled eggs.

" 'Ike,' I said, 'there are a whole lot of government horse right there in your corral.' Ike looks right at me and says 'They must've wandered in last night off the prairie an mixed in with ours.' " Ben Moon shook his head and of fered a smile.

"So I tell Ike he is under arrest and he asks why and I
l him for stealing horses but if there were laws against
ing dumb I'd arrest him for that as well." ·

Ben Moon tapped his empty glass on the bar and the
rtender refilled it.

"That was when Billy stepped between Ike and me. He
rted jawing about how I had no right to arrest Ike. I told
m to give it a rest. He drew his piece, and I shot him.
e bullet whistled through Billy and found Ike. Killed him
ne-dead. It was the damndest thing."

"Well, it sounds like he had it coming," said Ned.

"At first I thought so, too," said Ben Moon, staring into
e amber whorls of his glass. "But looking back on it, I'm
t so sure. Ike wasn't all that terrible a person. He just
ppened to get unlucky."

Ned said he was hungry and insisted that they find a
staurant.

"You go eat," said Ben Moon. "I'm going to ask around
out Doc Pierce."

"We stay here long," said Ned Bluecorn, "we'll just be
king for trouble from that city marshal and his bunch."

"I wouldn't worry too much about Billy," said Ben Moon.
le's not dumb enough to let me shoot him twice."

Ned found a restaurant and ate three sandwiches and sev-
al pickles and waited for Ben Moon to show up. He had
lark feeling about Dodge, about Billy Tibbs and his depu-
·s. It was the only Indian thing left to him, his intuition.

It didn't take long to learn that Doc Pierce had been in
odge—not more than two weeks previously. And yes, he
d been accompanied by a young, pretty woman with dark-
d hair. Doc had bragged that he was heading to Denver.

Ben Moon found Ned Bluecorn inspecting a large pickle
held between his finger and thumb.

"Have you ever seen a pickle this big?" he asked.

"Doc was here in Dodge," said Ben Moon, "but has sinc left."

"What about Sarah?"

"It sounds like she's still with Doc."

"Jane would be disappointed to know that her child ha gone off with a professional gambler," said Ned Bluecor sliding one end of the pickle into his mouth.

"She doesn't need to know," said Ben. "Let's go." H decided they'd take the north road again and stop in Hay to check on Jane's condition before turning west towar Colorado.

Ned Bluecorn had purchased a whole fried chicken an casually gnawed on it as they rode.

"I am glad to be out of Dodge," he said between bite.

"Don't you ever get full?" asked Ben Moon.

"No," said the Indian flatly.

They rode until dusk, found a small tributary, and fo lowed it off the main road until they made camp.

There was a gentle wind from the west, and the sky sof ened to a pale rose color. They unsaddled their horses an hobbled them so they could graze and then tossed the bedrolls down.

Ned ate the last of the chicken and threw the bones awa

Ben Moon sat cross-legged and smoked a cigarette. " could stand some coffee," he said. "You didn't buy an coffee did you?"

"No. Just this chicken. It was all that I had money fo and it looked pretty good." Ned Bluecorn sat with his leg straight out and his back against his saddle. He watched cricket that had crawled up onto his boot. "Denver's a lor way," he said.

"Far enough."

Several moments of silence passed between them.

"I was thinking that by the time we track down the gambler and find Sarah . . ."

"Jane will have died."

"Yes. That is what I was thinking."

"What if she's dead by the time we get back to Hays?" emanded Ned. "What will you do if she has already ied?"

"Do about what?"

"About finding the girl."

"I don't know," said Ben Moon, watching the first star f the new night and letting the quiet stretch into silence. ach man weighed his own thoughts.

"There's something maybe I ought not to tell you," said ed Bluecorn, his voice low and dark as the sky.

"Well, then don't."

"It's something I've been thinking about ever since we arted out."

"Ned, if there is something that you want to say, then ay it; if not, I'd just as soon go to sleep."

"It's something that I know, but I don't think I'm supposed to know. That's why I'm having a hard time deciding n whether to tell you or not."

"You're goddamn mysterious, Ned. I'll say that for you. reckon all Indians are. More so than white men."

"I think Jane would be damn mad at me if I told you."

"Then, as I said, keep it to yourself."

"Maybe so," said Ned, lying down and resting his head pon his saddle. He reached for his cover and drew it up ver him.

Ben Moon banked the small fire they had built and rolled p in his own blanket. He was nearly asleep when Ned said, Jane's daughter has got your blood in her."

Ben Moon didn't speak for a time, and Ned thought th
he was already asleep. He felt foolish for talking to himse
in the dark. *Well, maybe it was something that he shou
keep to himself after all.*

"Who told you that?" asked Ben Moon after several mi
utes.

"I overheard."

"From whom?"

"I overheard Jane telling Sassy one day shortly befo
she got it in her head to find the girl."

"You knew the whole while and didn't tell me?"

"I figured if Jane wanted you to know, she would ha
told you herself."

He tried to think back. Eighteen years ago was a lo
time to remember. At first he denied the possibility. *Whe
in the hell had he been eighteen years ago. Where had Ja
been?*

Abilene. They had both been in Abilene eighteen yea
ago. They had been keeping regular company. Abilene w
when he had come close to asking her to marry him.

It was possible.

An hour more passed. A pack of coyotes had caug
something not far away, a rabbit perhaps, and yipped a
cried and howled over their prey.

The flames of the fire licked at the black stillness. T
quarreling coyotes settled their dispute and fell silent. N
Bluecorn watched a shooting star streak across the sky a
felt the dullness of sleep creep through his brain.

"You should have said something before now," were t
last words he heard Ben Moon say.

Sixteen

Word was, Ben Moon was in Lost River.

Word was, Ben Moon was living with a dying whore in a big house.

Word was, that Ben Moon was going blind from syphilis and that his hands shook so badly from booze somebody had to hold his glass for him.

Killing Ben Moon would be easy!

Sam Pepper wore a fringed jacket and a beaver hat and rode a high-stepping stud. Faces turned to stare at the man who rode down the middle of their street.

Even though it was a spring day, it was spitting snow and the stud's hooves shattered thin plates of ice that had formed over puddles and ruts.

The man on the strutting horse did not go unnoticed by Tom Cooly, Lost River's only peace officer.

Tom Cooly was dressed in a long heavy coat with a curly sheepskin collar dyed black. The coat came down past his boot tops. He wore a sugar-loaf Stetson with the brim curled up and kidskin gloves that didn't seem warm enough, even though it was *spring*.

The man on the stud seemed not to take notice of the man in the long coat standing beneath the gray-and-green awning in front of the hardware store.

Sam Pepper turned the stud's head in at the town's only

restaurant. He dismounted, and when he did, the saddl
leather creaked under his weight.

He paused long enough to look up and down the stre
in both directions then stepped inside the eatery.

He smelled something good in the air—something frie

A man wearing a denim jacket and a wool scarf aroun
his neck looked up from the plate of food in front of hin
He had small round eyes, like those of a rodent, and saggin
pink cheeks lined with tiny blue veins. When Sam Pepp
stared back, the man's eyes returned to his food.

A table near the window seemed to suit him; the plat
glass was shrouded in steam, and he wiped away a circl
so that he might see out.

A woman approached; she wore an apron of muslin an
had small feet.

"You are new in town," she said.

"I've just arrived," said Sam Pepper. She felt uneas
about his stare, but thought him masculine and strong i
the face.

"What will you have?"

"What is your specialty?" he asked.

He seemed to smile when he said it, but she could n
be certain.

"Cowboy hash and fried potatoes," she said. "Lots
our customers prefer it. The beefsteak is pretty good, too

He nodded his assent.

It was then that the man in the long dark coat entere
the restaurant. Sam Pepper took notice.

The man's approach was slow and deliberate

"You are Sam Pepper," the man said, stopping a few fe
from the table.

"Have we met somewhere before?"

"No, but I know who you are. I know that you are from Denver, and I know all about your reputation."

"Well now, mister, that is an awful lot to know," said Sam Pepper, feeling the muscles of his gut tighten beneath his belt buckle.

Then the man pulled open the coat far enough to reveal a sawed-off shotgun resting along one leg, suspended by a long piece of rawhide.

"It's twelve gauge in case you are wondering. I sometimes load it with dimes."

Sam Pepper saw, too, the badge the man was wearing pinned to his shirt pocket. It had a dull gleam to it and was the size of a silver dollar.

"You have mistaken me for trouble," said Sam Pepper.

"I don't know how else to figure it," said Tom Cooly. "A man like you shows up in Lost River; it can't be because of our weather. I'd like you to clear out."

"I haven't had my meal yet."

"You're welcome to eat it, then clear out."

Tom Cooly let his finger rest on the twin triggers of the shotgun. It wouldn't take more than swinging it upwards and cutting loose. Both men could see that.

Tom Cooly waited to see if he would have to use the shotgun. The idea of shooting it out with the infamous Sam Pepper was only a little troubling; he figured the shotgun weighed heavily in his favor.

"You're making a mistake."

"If you want to settle it here and now, go ahead."

The lawman's gaze was even, unflinching. The woman who had taken Sam Pepper's order stood a few feet away holding a plate of steaming cowboy hash.

"I'll leave," said Sam Pepper. "All I came in for was to eat, like everyone else."

"I'll be outside, Mr. Pepper. You've got fifteen minutes."

He watched the man in the long coat back his way to the door and then step outside. The woman set the plate down in front of him and said, "You must be somebody!"

"Is there a whorehouse in this town?" asked Sam Pepper.

The woman's eyes grew large and her face flushed crimson. Drawing herself up stiffly, she said, "Everyone knows there is."

"Where?"

"West of the town, just outside the limits. If it were not Constable Cooly would have shut it down a long time ago. It is not a place where decent men would go."

"You'd be surprised," said Sam Pepper.

He found the place easily enough. It was a large, two story house with painted gables and shutters on the windows and a porch that held a swing on each end. It had the commanding presence of a courthouse or an opera theater.

He stepped unto the porch, scraping mud from the bottoms of his boots as he did so.

Before knocking, he drew the Remington pistol and held it behind his back. If Ben Moon were unlucky enough to answer the door, he'd get a face full of lead. He banged twice before the door opened. A black man with long graceful fingers stood before him.

"It's too early for bidness," said the black man. "Gals don't start working till after evening. Miss Jane's rules. Miss Jane says a man that can't wait till after evening for his pleasure is either a sinner or a cowboy."

"I'm looking for someone."

"Ain't no one here but me," said the black man.

"I'm looking for a man named, Ben Moon."

"Yas, suh. Ben Moon."

"Is he around?"

"No, suh. Ben Moon ain't been around for a while."

Sam Pepper brought the pistol around and showed it to the black man.

"I ain't fooling."

"No, suh. I didn't think you was."

"When's the last time you seen Ben Moon?"

The black man shrugged his shoulders, rolled eyes the color of bloody egg yokes, and scratched his bony skull with one of the long graceful fingers.

"I guess it'd be when him and Miss Jane and the others all went to Kansas to find Miss Jane's baby girl."

"When?"

"Ten, fifteen days ago. Maybe longer."

"I could shoot you in the face and nobody would even care," said Sam Pepper.

"Yas, suh. I reckon you could, and I reckon they wouldn't. I'm only a piano player."

"A damn lucky one today," said Sam Pepper, lowering the pistol.

"Where'd he live?"

"Who's that?"

"Ben Moon. The man I've been talking about."

"Oh, Mistuh Moon stays out by himself in a Chinaman's shack near the river. Least he did before him and Miss Jane left."

"Which way?"

"That," said the black man pointing to the south road leading away from the big house.

"I might be back," said Sam Pepper. "If you're lying, I'll come back and shoot you. Do you understand that?"

"Yas, suh. I believe you would."

* * *

Tom Cooly ate his supper at home, across the table from his wife and children. For the most part, they ate in silence except for the children who had a tendency to chatter until the faded blue gaze of their father came to rest on them. He chewed at his food with a look of consternation in his otherwise handsome face.

"Your job has gotten the better of you," said Tom Cooly' wife, Zeralda. She had dark hair and eyes as brown as those of a doe. She had a round, cheerful face and had grown bottom-heavy from bearing the children. He remembered her as once having been thin.

"There was a man in town today," he said, lifting a fork ful of peas to his mouth. "His name is Sam Pepper. He i a known shootist and has killed plenty of men."

"What's he doing here?" Zeralda's brown eyes turned sat urnine.

"I didn't trouble to ask. I ordered him to leave."

"I'm glad you did, Tom. We don't need men like tha here. It was bad enough to have Ben Moon in our midst I am glad he is gone as well."

Zeralda sighed one of her great sighs that seemed to le all the air out of her bosom. The bodice of her gingham dress rose and fell, and then she bent her head in order t eat what was on her fork.

Tad, Tom Cooly's oldest son, asked, "What is a shootist? And Ben, the younger child, asked, "Who is Ben Moon?

"Hush," said Zeralda, "and eat your food."

"Ben Moon wasn't so bad," said Tom Cooly. "He neve gave me, nor anyone else, trouble in spite of his reputation.

"It is said that he once shot a man for snoring," whis pered Zeralda as she spooned some brown sugar over bowl of mush.

"Do you children want some?" she asked.

"I have heard that story, too," said Tom. "I don't believe everything I hear."

"You know the sort of man he is," said Zeralda. "He consorts with that harlot, Jane . . . whatever her last name is. It is said that they are lovers and that he has killed men because of her."

Tom Cooly shook his head.

"Is that all you and those other women do, tell gossip?" Her cheery face lost its smile.

"Everyone knows what that woman is. It's no secret. And Ben Moon is no secret either. People like that are just plain trash."

Tom Cooly glanced at the wide-eyed faces of his children.

"I think we have talked enough about Ben Moon and that woman and Sam Pepper. Our supper is getting cold."

"Fine," Zeralda said, stabbing a potato with her fork.

Tom Cooly finished his meal first and excused himself from the table.

"I need to go make my rounds," he said. He waited for Zeralda to say something kind, something understanding.

"Fine," she said, her eyes flashing her anger.

"Well, then, I'll be back shortly," he said apologetically. She and the children continued to eat, but watched him.

He put on his long coat and settled the sugar-loaf hat on his head before taking the shotgun that rested in the corner. Cradling it in the crook of one arm, he stepped out into the night air.

The town lay a hundred yards distance from the small clapboard house which he himself had built on a lot he had paid fifteen dollars for.

It was his house, his town. A good place to raise a family, a good place to live. He knew everyone and everyone knew

him. He had no enemies; everyone was a neighbor. It wa
a good place to maintain the law. Life was easy.

He made his rounds, rattling doorknobs to make sur
businesses were locked up. He checked the crowd a
Bellingham's Saloon; they were as peaceful as a congrega
tion on Sunday. He went past the livery and spoke a fev
words with Mike, the blacksmith, then moved on until h
reached the town's limits.

He could see lights on in the windows of the house sim
ply referred to as Jane's place, just beyond the town'
boundary. He saw horses and a few buggies tied up in th
front yard. He'd know, upon closer inspection, whom th
animals and carriages belonged to. But it didn't matter t
him. A man's personal business was his own.

Turning, he crossed the street and started down the othe
side and back toward his own home.

Nothing was wrong. He checked each door along th
way. Twisted the doorknobs, rattled them, peered in throug
the dark windows. Nothing was wrong.

One more block of buildings, and then he would be hom
again. Zeralda would be over her snit by now. Perhaps, afte
the children were asleep, he and she would find a little tim
together. It seemed like after little Ben was born Zerald
hadn't shown much interest in spending time together, n
in that way she hadn't.

Maybe tonight she would.

He stepped off the walk in order to pass in front of a
alleyway that separated the two sets of buildings.

He was thinking about Zeralda when something move
in the darkness of the alley.

He was thinking about Zeralda and turned to look int
the darkness.

"What . . ."

The answer came in a flash of light.

He felt something punch him in the chest.

"Oh!" It surprised him.

He felt himself floating. Then, he hit the ground hard. Someone stepped out of the dark and stood by his face. He tried to lift himself but was unable to move. He felt cold. He felt the earth tilting, felt himself sliding off the edge.

"Am . . . I shot?" he muttered, the mud bubbling up around his mouth as he spoke. He could taste the mud on his tongue.

"Yes," said the figure whose boots were inches from his face.

"Were you the one?" asked Tom Cooly.

"I told you earlier you were making a mistake. Now you know," said the figure.

"Sam Pepper?"

The boots turned slowly and walked away.

Tom Cooly took a deep breath and closed his eyes. *The angels will come soon,* he thought. His nostrils blew bubbles in the mud, then stopped.

Seventeen

Ben Moon fell asleep thinking about a child he had neve
known. She would be a woman now. It seemed strange. H
saw the glowing embers of the fire, listened to the silenc
of the night, felt the creeping blackness.

Billy Tibbs and his deputies approached the campsit
carefully.

"There those sons of bitches are," he said to the other
as they sat their horses a hundred yards distance from th
dying campfire.

Ned Bluecorn was dreaming of Jane. In his dream, Jan
was young and beautiful and full of health. She smiled a
him the way a woman smiles at a man she's interested in

"What's the point of our being here, Billy?" asked Sila
Odell, a lean leathery man with great flowing silver mus
taches.

"As far as I'm concerned," said Marshal Billy Tibb
"those men are desperados. We need to clean the land c
their kind."

"We could just as easily have arrested them earlie
couldn't we?"

"Shut up, Silas. This ain't a point to be debated."

"What *is* the point, Billy?"

Billy Tibbs couldn't see Silas Odell's clear gray eyes i

the dark, but he knew them to be obstinate. Without bothering to answer, Billy turned his attention to the others.

"The way I see it, we surround their camp and fire in on them. Men like that, you don't give a chance to surrender."

There was a silence as deep as the night among them.

"We'll leave the horses here and approach on foot. Spread out. Silas, since you don't show much willingness to carry out your official duties, you stay here and hold the reins."

Silas Odell grunted and spat.

Ned Bluecorn turned over in his sleep, pulling the bedroll up over him as he did.

The first slug spanked up dust from his blanket. Ben Moon came awake instantly at the sound of gunfire. His hand reaching for the Starr, he pushed off his blankets.

Too late! Something hard and painful drove into his side. And then something tore through his upper leg. He fired the Starr until the hammer clicked on empty cartridges. He was reaching for more shells, reaching down, feeling the spread of blood from his wounds, when his head seemed to explode.

The rapid return-fire from the camp withered the resolve of Billy Tibbs and his men, and the battle scene fell silent.

"What now, Billy?" questioned a deputy.

"I say we get in the wind," said another. "This is bad business what we've done here tonight, Billy."

He detested them for their faintheartedness.

"Remind me to look for new help when we get back," he said through clenched teeth.

He could hear their boots crunching ground as they retreated to their horses. He thought about going into the camp alone and making sure the job was finished. Then,

he thought about Ben Moon maybe lying there waiting fo
him to come and felt his own resolve weaken.

"Well, I guess whatever you got, you son of a bitch," he
shouted toward the camp, "you had coming!" He had begun
to sweat even though the night air had turned cold. He heard
the others calling him to come on. With a mixture of re
luctance and relief, he went.

Something hot burned his face. Flies swarmed over his
blood-caked head. With much effort, he was able to open
his eyes. His head pounded with pain; his left side and leg
were on fire.

He took slow deep breaths and tried to stir the fog from
his mind. He was hurt. Shot. He wanted to move, felt like
he couldn't, forced himself to. His blood had stained the
ground. He found the Starr, inches away from his right
hand. He reached for it, drew it near. A mixture of dirt and
blood and mucous clogged his nostrils and throat. He sat
up and swallowed several times in order to breathe easier.
He fought the sensation of dizziness, placed his good hand
on the ground to support himself.

Slowly, his mind began to clear.

Ned Bluecorn lay on the other side of the gray ashes o
their camp's fire. He had not moved.

"Ned . . ."

He looked up into the sky. Judging by the sun, it would
be late morning. Ned Bluecorn never slept much past dawn

"Ned!"

He knew without having to look that Ned Bluecorn was
dead. As best he could, he managed to cross the short dis
tance between them and draw back the blanket.

A small trickle of crusted blood had leaked from a blac

hole in the side of Ned Bluecorn's skull. Another had pierced his neck and left the collar of his shirt soaked and still wet.

"Jezzus, Ned. I don't know any words to say for you."

Ned had lost his bulk and size in death, as all men seemed to. His brown hands lay clasped in fists. His mouth was grim, as though death had been a bitter thing.

Ben Moon did the only thing he could for the Indian. He reached over and closed his eyes.

Still holding the Starr, he struggled to his feet, took a step, then fell. The wounded leg would not hold him.

"Damn it!" His curse sounded slight on the blowing wind.

It was Billy Tibbs, he told himself. Only Billy Tibbs would do a thing like this—shoot a man in his blankets!

He tore open his shirt and examined the wound in his side. It was sore and already bruising where the bullet had gone in. And where it had gone out. The wound had crusted over.

He turned his attention to the bloody, ragged hole in his leg. The leg was painful, the foot numb. Upon closer inspection, he could tell that the bullet was still inside and that maybe it had nicked a bone. He tested it, bit the inside of his cheek when he did, and lay back on the ground.

It was a damn poor fix he was in. Maybe Ned had been the lucky one.

Ned was wearing a blue bandanna around his neck; it wasn't doing him any good. Ben Moon reached over and removed it, soaked with blood as it was, and retied it around his leg.

When he had regained a measure of strength, he searched the camp, by crawling, and found one of their canteens. It had a single bullet hole in it but still contained a small portion of water.

It was the best-worst water he had ever drunk.

He looked around, could see nothing but prairie. Lots of prairie.

He couldn't eat prairie and he couldn't drink prairie; and if he couldn't do that, he couldn't live. And even if he could, the flies would blow his wounds full of maggots and gangrene would set in.

He smiled grimly.

"I never thought it'd end like this for us, Ned," he said to the lifeless form of the Indian.

"I always thought me and you would wind up killing each other. I guess, maybe, in a way, we have."

He looked down at the Starr in his hand. There was still one choice left to him.

He drank the last of the water and fell back from exhaustion.

The wagon came sometime later.

Kid Joe was the first to spot what appeared to be dead animals lying out on the prairie.

Kid Joe's daddy saw them, too. He "hawed" the team of horses forward, but at a cautious walk.

"It's two fellers," said Kid Joe as the wagon drew near.

"Dead men," said Joe's daddy.

"I reckon so, Pa. I wonder how they died out here?"

"No telling, Kid Joe. Men die all the time in all sorts of places."

The older man hauled back on the reins and the wagon rattled to a halt.

"You be careful there, Kid," he cautioned his son.

"I will, Pa," said Kid Joe, reaching behind the wagon seat for the Sharps carbine.

Kid Joe walked to the nearest of the bodies, a man whose hands were balled into fists. Kid Joe bent over in order to look more closely at the dead man.

"He looks Indian, Pa."

"Is he dead for sure?"

"Yes, sir. Shot through the bean and gizzard."

"Check the other one."

Kid Joe straightened, looked once at his daddy, then moved to the second body.

"What about him?" Kid Joe's daddy leaned over the side of the wagon and spat some of the plug tobacco juice that had pooled inside his mouth.

"He looks dead, too," said Kid Joe.

"Damn. That means we'll have to take time out of our sod-collecting and bury them. I hadn't counted on burying two fellers today," complained Kid Joe's daddy. "Come and get a spade."

Kid Joe stared into the face of the second man, a man who looked old enough to be his daddy's age. He had a bloody hole in his side and another in his leg. Kid Joe noticed, too, the Starr revolver in the man's hand. It had fancy grips. He took it and stuck it in his belt.

They labored over the digging of two shallow graves; several times Kid Joe's daddy, a man everyone knew as Fess Foley, had to take a blow and rest on the handle of his shovel.

"Why not just dig one grave, Pa, and put 'em both in it?" Kid Joe didn't appreciate the extra work.

"Judging from the looks of 'em," said Fess Foley, "these boys ain't never had much in their whole, dern lives. Look at the poor way they're dressed. Least we can do is give 'em their own graves."

The work even made Kid Joe sweat, but not as bad as
his daddy.

"Let's drop the Indian in first," said Kid Joe's daddy.
And, they did. They used Ned Bluecorn's bedroll as
shroud before shoveling in the fresh moist dirt over him.
took about five minutes. And when they had finished, the
patted down the mound with their spades.

"Go get the cider jug out of the wagon," said Fess Fole
"I've worked up a thirst."

It was busthead whiskey that left an aftertaste on th
tongue like kerosene, but Kid Joe's daddy fought it down
grimaced, and licked his lips.

"Don't ever fall prey to the demon rum, Kid. It'll hu
you going down and hurt you later on in life." Fess Fole
pounded the cork back into the mouth of the jug and set
down on the ground, making sure it was balanced an
wouldn't tip over.

"Well, I reckon we'd better drop that other feller in th
ground and get back to sod-cutting. You know how you
mam can be when we're late for her supper."

Kid Joe took the head and his daddy the feet, and wit
a great effort, they lifted the body up and dropped it int
the three-foot-deep grave.

Both men were amazed when the body moaned the
moved.

"Jezzus Kid, the sucker is alive!"

Kid Joe's mouth fell open and his eyes were as big
liberty dollars.

"Help me pull him out!"

Ben Moon struggled against the hands that were trou
bling him, that were lifting him and dropping him. He hea
voices. He managed to open his eyes, saw two faces wearir
straw hats.

They laid him on the ground. Fess Foley pulled the cork from his cider jug and spilled some of the whiskey into the mouth of Ben Moon. It was enough to wear off the fog in his brain.

"We thought you dead," said Kid Joe's daddy.

Ben Moon stared into the man's frosty blue eyes.

"Somebody shot you through and through, mister," said Kid Joe. Ben Moon eyed the whiskey jug.

"Sure," said Fess Foley. And again he put the jug to Ben Moon's lips.

It tasted as mean as anything he had ever drunk, but it did the trick and his head cleared enough to speak.

"I need help, mister."

"That's plain to see, friend. How'd this happen?"

Kid Joe examined the place on Ben Moon's scalp that had been seared by a bullet. It was a bloody track as long as two of his fingers.

"I'd feel more inclined to talk about it once these holes get plugged up," said Ben Moon. "Everything's leaking out of me."

"Sure, sure," said Fess Foley, tipping the cider jug to his own lips. "We got a place not far from here. Me and Kid. Take his topside, boy, and let's put him in the wagon."

They lifted him with great care and laid him on slabs of fresh-cut sod, but it still hurt like hell anyway.

"How far?" asked Ben Moon as soon as the wagon had bounced the first few hundred yards.

"Two, three miles," said Kid Joe. Every bounce and jolt of the spring wagon felt like a kick or a punch.

"Two or three miles . . ." muttered Ben Moon.

Eighteen

Somewhere in the space of two or three miles, Ben Moon journeyed to strange and frightening places. An apparition he knew as death appeared and whispered something cold into his ear. Ned Bluecorn's corpse cried out to him. Each time he felt the sting of bullets piercing his skin, he jolted awake and felt overcome by the sight of blue sky overhead by the voice of the two men on the wagon seat.

The wagon finally halted, and they lifted him out of it and carried him into a house made of sod. He heard the voices of women, saw their faces for a brief moment.

The conversation dulled in the roaring of his head. He was placed on a bed, and he could feel his clothes being cut off.

"Who is this stranger, Fess?" asked one of the women.

"Me and Kid Joe found him out on the prairie near where we were cutting sod, Martha. Him and this other feller, an Indian, we think, were shot to pieces. We buried the Indian."

"An Indian?" echoed the other woman.

"He wasn't no wild Indian," said Kid Joe. "He was dressed about like this feller—like a white man." Kid Joe remembered how the Indian's hands were squeezed into fists as though he were angry about dying.

"Lord, he's a mess," said the woman Martha as Ben Moon felt his clothes being cut from him.

"Get some water and heat it on the stove, Pearl," directed the woman.

He heard the two women whispering as they washed his naked skin with warm, wet cloths.

"Don't be bashful child," said Martha. "You've seen naked men before."

"But not strangers, Mama."

"Wash his neck, then. And his arms. I'll do the rest."

Their washing was slow and gentle, their hands like those of angels, their voices soothing. He winced when they began to clean his wounds.

Afterwards, the men came back into the room—Fess and Kid Joe.

"Is he still with us?" asked Fess Foley. The women had washed the dirt and crusty blood away, revealing the stranger's blanched skin. They had dressed his wounds with white strips of linen. And they had washed and shaved his face and neck.

"I don't know if being clean helps his chances any," said Martha Foley. "But it can't hurt."

"With his beard shaved off, he don't look near so worn out," said Kid Joe.

Kid Joe's sister, Pearl, was trying to fill up her mind with things other than the remembered glimpses she had stolen of the naked stranger in spite of her embarrassment.

"We've done all we can," said Martha Foley. "It's up to higher powers than ours whether he will make it or not."

"You're right, woman," said her husband. "All we can do now is eat our supper and go to bed. If that feller's still alive come morning, I'll be surprised."

After supper, Kid Joe and Pearl took their beds outside the soddy because there was too little room for all five of them to sleep inside.

"It's dern chilly," said Kid Joe, slipping beneath his blankets.

Pearl studied the stars.

"Do you think that man is dangerous?" she asked.

"I dunno." Kid Joe said. "Maybe he is. He was in a shootout, all right. Most folks don't get into shootouts."

"And the fellow with him was murdered."

"He sure was. Shot to pieces. Worst thing I've ever seen."

"A desperado?"

"Maybe so. I took a Starr from his hand. No ordinary man would carry so elegant a pistol."

"Do you reckon he robs the rich and helps the poor?"

"You're a fanciful thinker, Pearl."

"Shot down in a daring encounter with those who would have him dead . . ."

"You've been reading pa's *Police Gazette,* haven't you Pearl? If pa catches you, he'll whip the skin off your butt."

Pearl Foley had already decided that the strange, wounded man inside their soddy was a mysterious marauder of the plains, a savior of women and orphans, a bank robber who would see that the looted bounty landed in the hands of the needy. She fell asleep already dreaming.

Time had passed. How long, Ben Moon couldn't say. He opened his eyes at one point and was fully awake. A woman sat next to his bed. She was young and attractive with honey-colored hair and fox-brown eyes.

She presented a tight smile when he looked at her.

"You have returned to us," she said.

The room was warm and dry, and a bright blade of sunlight stabbed through the open window above his bed. He tried to speak, found he couldn't because of the dryness in his throat. She poured water into a tin cup and held it for him to sip.

"Who—"

"I'm Pearl. My pa and brother found you out on the prairie shot full of holes. No one thought you'd live. No one except me."

He lifted himself on one elbow, felt a deep ache in his side, another coursing up from his leg. He was wearing a nightshirt. His leg was splinted with cottonwood limbs.

"I had a friend . . ."

"We know. Pa and Kid Joe buried him where they found him. They come close to burying you, too. But, when they tossed you into the grave, you made a fuss." Her smile was nervous.

He remembered now. Remembered that Ned Bluecorn had been killed in his own blankets. Remembered thinking that the man responsible was Billy Tibbs. With great effort, he sat all the way up and, using both hands, swung his leg out of bed.

"Where are my clothes, sis?"

"Ma burned them. They were so smelly and bloody."

"Pearl, is that you chattering back there?" It was her ma from beyond the hung blanket that made a room of one portion of the soddy.

"Ma. The stranger's awake."

The blanket was pulled back, and an older version of the younger woman appeared.

"How do, mister. I'm Martha Foley."

"I need to get dressed," said Ben Moon.

"Whatever for?"

It was a good question. He didn't know why. He just felt the urgent need to get dressed and get moving.

"In case you ain't noticed, you've got a busted leg, a hole in your side, and a nice new way to part your hair. I'd

say you'd be better off waiting until you healed some before
you go traipsing off."

He felt trapped.

"Could you stand some victuals?"

The thought of food made him weak.

"How long have I been here?" he asked.

"Nearly ten days. You ought to eat."

Pearl brought him soup with beans and ham chunks in
it and black pieces of bread. The first few bites of food
made him nauseous, but he swallowed it down and finished
two more bowls of the thick, salty soup. He washed it down
with several glasses of goat's milk and heard the nanny
bleating outside. The goat's milk was thick and sweet.

Afterwards, he lay back, surprised at how exhausting it
had been just to eat a meal. He craved a cigarette.

"Did you find any tobacco in the pockets of my clothes?"
he asked.

"Found some makings," said the woman Martha. "But
they was all soaked in blood and so I pitched them out.
But Fess has got a extry pipe I reckon he wouldn't mind
you smoke, if you'd care."

"I'd find the chance to have a smoke right now an un-
common pleasure."

They helped him outside, a woman under each arm, and
set him in a chair, propping his poor leg up on an overturned
washtub. Pearl brought him the pipe and tobacco and asked
"Is the air too fresh for you?"

"No. It's just fine," he said. There was a dancing wind
that blew from west to east and smelled as clean as the
fresh-washed sheets the women had hung on wire lines to
dry. The sky was as bright and clear blue as he could ever
recall having seen it. There were horses in a corral, and
they came near the fencing and eyed him and pricked up

their ears and flared their nostrils at the smell of his tobacco smoke. They looked like good horses.

He watched the women working the clothes on the line—taking down the dry ones, hanging up wet ones. They were attractive women in a frontier sense: They had possessive smiles and happy eyes. Most of their kind reflected the rigors of frontier living in stark gazes and down-turned mouths. Not these women.

Pearl tossed him glances over her shoulder. He couldn't imagine what her interest in him might he.

Later, they brought him a mug of hot coffee and asked him if he would like some sugar in it.

"How can I refuse?" he said.

They brought him some biscuits as well, and he took his time chewing them and sipping the hot coffee. For a time, he let his chin fall to his chest and the warm sun put him to sleep. The rattle of a wagon and a team of approaching horses awakened him.

Kid Joe and Fess Foley climbed down from the wagon, introduced themselves, and offered their hands in friendship.

"It looks like you have come back to the living," said Fess Foley.

"I reckon you'll be wanting your Starr back," said Kid Joe, pulling the pistol from his belt. "I took it off you when we found you. I only meant to keep it because I thought you were . . ." He held it out for Ben Moon to take.

Ben Moon studied it for a long time, as if Kid Joe were holding a snake in his hand. Slowly, he reached out and took the Starr and immediately felt its heaviness.

"That's some pistol," said Kid Joe. "I like the fancy grips." Kid Joe's earnest gaze stayed fixed on the pistol.

"I've got some whiskey in the house if you'd care for a

shot," said Fess Foley. "You look like a man that might no[ ]
mind a taste of whiskey."

"Mister," said Ben Moon, "it's been a long time sinc[ ]
I've sipped whiskey. I wouldn't mind at all."

They stayed outside the whole day, Ben Moon and Fes[ ]
Foley drinking whiskey and smoking pipes while Kid Jo[ ]
sat on the ground Indian-style and listened to the two me[ ]
talk. The women kept busy with their wash and then wen[ ]
on to make lye soap and later killed a pair of chickens an[ ]
dipped them in a tub of hot water in order to pluck out th[ ]
feathers more easily.

Ben Moon felt his life beginning to come back.

They ate supper in silence; and afterwards, while th[ ]
women cleared the table, Ben Moon, with Fess Foley an[ ]
Kid Joe's help, sat outside and smoked some more and fin[ ]
ished off the last of the whiskey jug.

"It ain't none of my business," said Fess Foley, "but I'n[ ]
curious as to what led up to me and Kid finding you an[ ]
that other fellow out on the prairie all shot to ribbons."

"Just poor luck, I guess," said Ben Moon.

"It would have to be more than poor luck, I suspect. Ar[ ]
you the law? A bounty hunter?"

"No."

Pearl could hear her pa asking the man questions throug[ ]
the open window. He was being mysterious, just as she ha[ ]
suspected a man like him would be.

"You say your name is Ben Moon. It seems to me I'v[ ]
heard of you somewhere . . . heard that name."

It always came to this, he thought. *The name, the repu[ ]tation. It seemed that no matter how long ago he had earne[ ]it or how hard he had since tried to leave it behind him[ ]it dogged him.*

He stared off toward the last wink of sun as it slippe[ ]

beyond the edge of the prairie, the sky above it turning the color of roses.

Then it dawned on Fess Foley where he had heard the name *Ben Moon*.

"Say! I read about you in the *Police Gazette*. You're *that* Ben Moon!"

Now that his daddy said it, Kid Joe recalled it, too.

"Ben Moon," he said, his large front teeth flashing in the faded light. He said it like a whispered prayer.

Pearl heard the name, heard the way her daddy and Kid Joe spoke it. Her mind ran wild trying to remember if *she* had ever read anything in her father's *Police Gazette* about Ben Moon. She had not. But still, she had been right about him all along: He was a Mysterious Knight of the Plains!

"I'd appreciate my privacy," said Ben Moon.

It was the kind of mistake a family that had come west from Pennsylvania might make, bringing up a man's past, like that.

"I understand, Mr. Moon. We both do, don't we, Kid?"

Kid Joe nodded his head. "Yes sir, Mr. Moon. I didn't mean no disrespect."

"Well, the night's gotten old," said Fess Foley, stretching his arms a little too exaggeratedly and yawning a little too loudly.

"I reckon we ought to retire and let you get your rest; you've had a full day."

Later, that night, he heard Fess Foley whispering the secret to his wife. "That's Ben Moon, Martha. The *Police Gazette* reported that he killed more men than even Claude Highsmith. Fact is, *he*'s the one that *killed* Claude Highsmith."

"Why did you bring him here, then?" he heard the woman whisper back.

"Hell, do you think I would've if I'd known."

"Lord, what do we do now?"

"I don't know, Martha. I just don't know."

Nineteen

"Sassy, will you go to the telegraph office and see if there is any word from Ben?" The girl had been eating a plum and staring out the window of Jane's room. It had grown warm enough in the daytime to open the window and allow fresh air in.

"I knew from the minute we began," said Sassy, cupping the palm of her hand under the sweet fruit to catch the juice, "that those two couldn't be trusted. They have probably gone off with your money and gotten drunk and thrown in jail!"

"Do you always have to be so quarrelsome, child?"

"No, ma'am. I just know what I know."

The weeks had been a healing one for Jane. Slowly, ever so slowly, the pneumonia had left her, and in spite of lungs that felt weaker than ever before, she had begun to feel a renewal of spirit if not of strength.

She had lived through the worst of it.

"Before you go," she said. "Help me to the chair so that I may see what Hays, Kansas, looks like in the sunshine." She watched as Sassy laced up her shoes, taking an inordinate amount of time in doing so. The girl could be as impudent and balky as a sore-mouthed mule, but she was not without her own certain charm. Her smile alone could warm a room. And of her loyalty there was no doubt.

Jane had long since made up her mind that if Sarah coul
not be found, then Sassy would inherit her daughter's shar
of the legacy. For the past seven years, Sassy had, unknow
ingly, filled the role of daughter for her.

"Should I be stopping at the marketplace as well?" aske
Sassy, knowing full well that she should and taking a sma
basket from the table to prove it. She knew how Jane like
pears and O'Rilley's Grocery was rumored to have gotte
in a fresh shipment of fruits and vegetables.

"Whatever you think is best," said Jane, pleased to b
sitting by the window where the sun could warm her an
the air smelled fresh.

Sassy was always happy to go shopping. Miss Jane woul
give her money which she could spend however she chos
And then, of course, there was that Corbett boy with th
flaming red hair down at Tuggle's Harness Shop that alway
took notice of her whenever she lingered out front.

Lately, he had been so bold as to ask her to meet hir
down by Dancer's Creek after the sun went down. Naturall
she had refused, which made him ask all the more, whic
made her want all the more to meet him—but not so quickl
as to seem wild or wicked.

"You're just a randy ol' white boy," she had teased. Sh
watched with great glee as his face flushed as red as hi
hair and his green eyes rolled while he toed at the groun
with his foot.

She stopped first at the telegrapher's office, hoping upo
hope that there wouldn't be any word from Ben Moon o
that ugly Indian as to their whereabouts. If they never di
come back, it would be too soon for her.

The telegrapher shook his head when asked about mes
sages, which set just fine with her.

She wandered along the sidewalk, pausing to star

through the plate-glass windows of the stores, especially the ones that had ladies' dresses and ladies' hats and ladies' shoes. The hardware store didn't interest her, nor did the gun shop, nor the tobacconist in front of which there were several ill-defined gentlemen standing. They cast her curious looks as she passed by; and, without looking left nor right, she heard one of them say, "Prissy little thing for a colored girl."

She dared not stop!

She hurried past the saloons and the billiard halls, knowing that more vile creatures lurked inside those devil's dens.

A Celestial stood in front of his laundry, sweeping a broom back and forth. When she approached, he paused and gave her a wide grin that showed several spiked teeth and said, "How do, Missy." He looked like a grinning jack-o-lantern. She hurried on without returning the greeting.

She crossed the street and passed slowly in front of the harness shop. Coyly, she glanced inside. The light was dim, and the strong scent of leather permeated the air. It was a smell she found pleasing. *Where was that Jud Corbett, anyway? She couldn't just stop and stand there as if she were waiting for him, could she?* Most days, he was hanging out front as if he were waiting for her to come by, and most days she did. But now, this day, when she wanted him to be out front, he was nowhere to be seen.

Well, phooey on him! She marched, in small quick steps that had her heels clicking on the boards, straight on down to O'Rilley's Grocery Store and picked out the best brown pears and the sweetest, largest red apples that she could find. They cost two dollars, but they filled her basket and she didn't care a bit.

A tall man on a bald-faced horse rode by and stared at her for a heartbeat. But in that moment he had looked at

all of her, and it sent a cold finger down her spine. Hi
looking at her had the same effect as Ned Bluecorn's stare—
or Ben Moon's. He was the same sort of man.

She hurried on, debating whether to cross the street agai
or make one last attempt to draw out the Corbett boy. Sh
surely was feeling spicy.

Sam Pepper took in an eyeful of the Negro gal; it ha
been a long time since he had *known* a woman of colo
She had averted her eyes the minute he looked her way. H
didn't mind a woman that was shy, but other business hel
his attention for the moment.

After having paid the black piano player a second vis
up in Lost River, he had learned that Hays—or somewher
in that vicinity—was where Ben Moon and the sick pros
titute had said they were going. Something to do with look
ing for a child.

At first, the old spade hadn't wanted to talk about it, bu
a good pop on the head with the barrel of his Remingto
had convinced him otherwise. Lots of men are willing t
talk when they're being busted on the head with iron.

Hays hadn't changed much since he had last seen it som
two years previously. He wondered if he still had friend
in town, one friend in particular—Jimmy Delgado, a far
dealer and pimp, a man who knew almost everything an
everybody.

He walked his horse down the center of Main Street, the
turned south across the railroad tracks that divided the tow
and into the "district."

Crib houses and dance halls, gambling parlors and opiur
dens. Just one row of buildings on either side of the dust

treet, but they were enough to fill any man's desire and to urn up all the money in his pockets.

Sam Pepper reined in in front of a false-fronted building ae remembered as the Cock's Tail. The new sign out front aid it was The Cowboy Club. It was where he had last nown Jimmy Delgado to ply his trade, to run his gals.

It was midday, the time of day when honest men were vorking, or at least thinking about it, the time of day when body could hear the buzz of flies in the air or his own reathing.

A man stood behind the bar drilling his pinky finger in is right ear. He offered an expectant look when Sam Pepper entered. The man had an officious face and waxed mustaches and wore a full-front white apron.

"How do, and welcome to The Cowboy Club, best saloon n the district."

Sam Pepper ordered a whiskey and a beer to chase it vith and watched as the man pulled down on the porcelain aandle until the beer streamed out like liquid gold and ormed a huge head of foam on top.

"Do you know a man named Jimmy Delgado?" Sam asked sipping the whiskey.

"J.D.? Sure."

"Do you know where I might find him?"

"Your best chance would be on down the way, over near he crib houses. He runs a few whores, likes to drink a lot, and gets mean. Deals faro every now and then."

"That's Jimmy. Thanks for the information." He paid the man six bits for the drinks and headed toward the cribs.

There was two rows of cribs, simple box affairs big enough for a whore to throw her pallet down either to do ousiness or sleep. He found a shack out back, a trickle of smoke rising from its stove pipe.

He banged hard on the door and stepped aside. He hea[r]
a shuffling inside and a man and a woman talking.

"Who's there?" The voice was that of a man, but hi[s]
squeaky, similar to that of a woman.

"Name's Sam Pepper. I'm looking for J.D., Jimmy D[el]
gado."

The shack was silent.

"I don't know no Sam Pepper."

"The hell you don't! Get out here, Jimmy; I need to a[sk]
you something."

It took all of a full minute for the door to creak open [on]
its hinges and for its inhabitant to make an appearance.

If it weren't for the long, slender fingers and the co[al]
black eyes, Sam Pepper might not have recognized Jimm[y]
Delgado. His skin was pocked with scabbed-over sores, a[nd]
most of his teeth were gone. A nervous tic pulled at o[ne]
side of his face, and he had lost a good fifty pounds.

"Sam . . ."

A woman appeared behind the man, her hair a tangl[e]
bush, her small round eyes searching and curious. She w[as]
a young woman, hardly more than a girl.

"Who's that, J.D.? Who's that feller? You ain't goin' [off]
somewhere are you? You ain't goin' off and leavin' me he[re]
alone, Jimmy . . ."

"Shut up, Philomena." The command came out soundi[ng]
like someone hawking up their phlegm.

"Sam, what'ya doin' here in Hays?"

"Looking for you, J.D."

"Well, hell. I guess you found me. Do you want to com[e]
in?"

"No, why don't you step out so's I can talk to you?"

"Jimmy, you ain't goin' off are you?" The woman w[as]
thin-boned, and her worn dress clung to her body.

"No, damn it! I'm just goin' to talk is all. He's a friend of mine. Get on back inside, will ya!"

Jimmy Delgado wasn't wearing shoes, and he stepped lightly from the stoop of the door to the hard-packed ground.

"I'm sorry you caught me unaware, Sam. This ain't how I usually live."

"Save the lies, Jimmy. I did not come to judge you. I come to ask you if a man's been through here lately."

"Who's the man?"

"Ben Moon."

Jimmy Delgado shifted his weight from foot to foot and hugged himself. He wore only a pair of stiff trousers and a shirt that was threadbare at the elbows.

"Ben Moon!"

"Talk has it he's down this way, down here around Hays. He's with a sick prostitute," said Sam Pepper, "and looking for a lost child."

"I heard Ben Moon died a year or two ago in Wyoming or Montana."

"You heard wrong, Jimmy. He's gonna die; he ain't dead yet."

Jimmy Delgado offered a weak, toothless smile, that of a sick man.

"You're on a job, ain't you?"

"Have you heard tell of him being in the area?"

"You're gonna kill ol' Ben Moon. Sweet Jesus! How much are you gettin' paid to do it?"

"That's a personal matter. Is he here?"

"Ben Moon. . . . Son of a bitch knocked me in the head once, arrested me, and put me in the can for two days. I had to pay a fifty-dollar fine. I sure wouldn't mind seein' him get his."

Sam Pepper took five silver dollars from his pocke
Jimmy Delgado eyed the coins.

"Go on and take them, Jimmy. There yours if you te
me about Ben Moon being in town."

The hands were bony, the fingers cold as they lifted tl
coins from Sam Pepper's palm.

"I can't say he's been here, Sam. I did hear of a fello
riding through ten, fifteen days back. A stranger that the
were some rumors about. He was with a sick woman an
an Indun. Some said the fellow looked like a pistol fighte
But, as far as I know, the fellow didn't leave his nam
spread about. It could've been Moon."

"Is he still here?"

"I don't believe so. I heard that him and the Indun rod
out."

"What about the woman they was with?"

"I don't know. I didn't hear if she rode out with them c
not. It wasn't that big news. Folks ride in and out of her
every day."

"Is that it? Is that all you can tell me for five dollars?

Jimmy Delgado shrugged his bony shoulders, plunge
his hand with the silver dollars deep into his pants pocke
and took a side step as though to avoid the hard stare c
Sam Pepper.

"I reckon so," he said, his sisterly voice breaking.

"I'm damned disappointed, Jimmy. Damned disap
pointed."

Sam Pepper stood, his feet wide apart, his hands on hi
hips, the butt of his Remington exposed for Jimmy Delgad
to see.

"I need the money, Sam."

"I reckon I didn't get much for it, Jimmy. I reckon tha
you still owe me something."

Jimmy swallowed hard and flexed his neck and waggled s head as though trying to find something to say.

"I reckon you wouldn't mind my going inside and spend-g some time with the lady."

"Ah . . . Sam. Me and her just got married. She ain't in e business."

"She looks like she might have been, Jimmy. I ain't never nown you to not be with one whore or another."

"She ain't no more, Sam. She's a good gal . . ."

"No, Jimmy, you owe me. You can't just take a man's oney and expect him not to get something for it."

"Times is hard, Sam."

"I reckon so."

"We just got married, me and her."

"Don't start crying, Jimmy. Be a man about things."

Jimmy Delgado started to bring the hand with the money ut of his pocket. "I'll give you back your money, Sam. ere, go on and take it!"

"Too late, Jimmy. A bargain is a bargain."

"I'm askin' you not to go inside with her. I'm beggin' ou not to."

"Let it be a lesson learned, J.D.: Don't strike deals if ou're not willing to hold up your end of the bargain. nough said."

Afterwards, Sam Pepper stepped outside the shack and ulled on his fringed jacket and adjusted his beaver hat. mmy Delgado looked at him with the disconsolate eyes f a whipped hound.

"You didn't do too bad for yourself, Jimmy, even if she awful young. Here's a spare dollar. She was worth it," e said, flipping a standing liberty in the air. It landed at mmy's bare feet.

"There was a colored girl with them."

"What?"

"I forgot to mention that there was a colored girl w
that stranger and Indun and sick woman."

"Well, now, I reckon I got my money's worth after a
You take care of yourself and the missus, Jimmy. It loo
like you've got a fine start on life."

Jimmy Delgado wished more than anything he had a g
and could blow the head off Sam Pepper. He swallow
back the anger that had caused his eyes to tear and be
down and picked up the silver dollar. *Six dollars.*

He cussed the day he had ever met Sam Pepper.

Twenty

"Where are you going at such an hour, child?"

Sassy had thought Jane to be sleeping.

"I . . . I just thought I might go for a little walk."

"This late?"

She was hesitant to tell Jane about Jud Corbett or why she'd be meeting him at this hour of the evening and where: Dancer's Creek—in the dark! Miss Jane would just tell her what a fool she was to be meeting a boy that way.

"It's time for all decent women to be in bed, Sassy. You won't find nothing but trouble outside this door after dark."

She swallowed hard.

"I'm goin' to meet someone," she said.

"Whom?"

"A fella."

"Goodness, girl, why haven't you spoke up before now? Why haven't you told me that you've met a young man?"

"I guess I wasn't sure whether or not I liked him till now."

"I would think that if he thought proper of you, he'd come courting instead of asking you to sneak off in the middle of the night."

"He's a white boy, Miss Jane. He's afraid we'll be seen together and his daddy will have a conniption. You know how folks are."

Jane took a deep breath, surprised at her own stiff-necke
attitudes.

"Yes, Sassy. I do know how folks are. I guess my concer
is about your welfare out on the streets alone at night."

"I'll be all right. I promise."

"I reckon I can't keep you from going if your heart
set on it. And I guess you're old enough to do pretty muc
as you please. But, child, don't be taken in by some bo
you just met. Don't let your heart get broken."

Sassy stood by the bed and took one of Jane's warr
hands in her own.

"I'll be as good as cherry pie. I swear I will."

"You'll soon come to learn that men are hopeless crea
tures who promise you the moon and stars and deliver noth
ing more than heartache."

Sassy tittered and kissed Jane on the forehead and saie
"I guess it's something I will never know unless I first ge
started tryin' it."

"You are an impossible girl," said Jane. Sassy's brigh
smile reflected itself in her dark lovely face.

"If you are not back by midnight, I will summon the law
to go and look for you." The warning was barely noted a
Sassy stepped from the room and closed the door after he

A full moon gave her plenty of light to see by. Dancer
Creek was south of town, south of the railroad tracks, an
south of the "district." She had heard plenty of talk abou
the district, about its wickedness. The thought of having t
pass through that part of town both frightened and thrille
her.

But nothing frightened and thrilled her as much as th
thought of meeting Jud Corbett down by Dancer's Creek.

Be cautious, girl, she told herself as she stepped quickl
down the boardwalks, staying as much within the shadow

of the buildings as was possible. She reached the tracks, lifted her skirts to just above her ankles, and crossed over the twin ribbons of steel. The soles of her shoes crunched against the cinders, and she could smell the pungent creosote of the railroad ties.

Just beyond, she could see the glow of lights along the district's main street. Things were much livelier in this part of town than they were north of the tracks.

She could hear music—piano music—and laughter, the heavy Har! Har! of men's laughter, and the shriller eruptions of women. At one point, there was a crash of furniture and curses. She moved more quickly still.

She was only halfway through the district when, directly ahead, she spotted a quartet of men standing on the walk in front of one of the saloons. Their voices were loud, their talk rough and vulgar. She stopped within the deep shadow of a doorway.

She held her breath but was certain that her heart was beating so loudly that the men would soon hear it and find her out.

She waited for what seemed an interminably long time before the group broke up and reentered the saloon. Quickly, she scurried past the open doorway, a dark shadow in the yellow shaft of light and was beyond the buildings of the district. From there, it was a ten-minute walk to Dancer's Creek. She knew; she had gone there before and timed herself. Only now, Jud Corbett would actually be waiting for her.

She could hear the sliding water of the creek before she reached the edge of the cutbank. A stand of cottonwoods not yet in leaf clacked their bare branches in the wind.

The evening air had become a cold breath. She was glad

she had chosen to wear a cape—a heavy, black, wool cap
with red trim.

"Is that you, Sassy?" It was Jud Corbett, whisperin
loudly from near one of the trees.

"Who would you expect it to be?" she hissed, relieve
that she had made it through the district safely and feelin
suddenly more wicked than she could ever have imagine

She could see the redness of his hair even in the pa
light of the moon. He did not say anything for a time, b
she could hear his breathing, as if he had been running.

"Well, you sure don't act like you're happy I'm here,
she said. "I had to risk my very life traveling through th
district. I don't know what's got into my head lately. I swea
you make me think foolish thoughts!"

He swallowed hard, then stepped forward and kissed he

"There, does that prove how much I'm glad you're here?
he demanded.

It had been sudden and unexpected, and she never ha
been kissed by a boy before. She was surprised at how goo
it felt.

"Well, I reckon I wouldn't mind so much if you was
do that again," she said.

He did, this time longer than the time before. It mad
her feel tingly and left her breathless. "Oh my," she sai
and leaned against the trunk of one of the cottonwoods.

When she had managed to revive from this new pleasur
she said, "If your daddy knew what you were doin', he
skin you alive." Then she laughed and clapped her han
and spun around.

"Well, maybe," Jud Corbett agreed. "But, it'd be worth it.

"Do you mean it, Jud Corbett? Tell me you mean it th
I'd be worth gettin' skinned for!"

"Of course I mean it." He put both arms around her.

"Then why'd we have to meet in the dark clear down here away from town?" she asked, pulling back from his embrace. She knew she was being coy.

He tried to kiss her, but she pushed him away.

"You didn't answer my question, Jud Corbett.

He let her go.

"I swear, I don't understand," he said. "One minute you act glad to be here; the next, you're acting all flumoxed."

"I guess a woman has a right to change how she feels," she said. Then, it was his turn to be surprised as she grabbed him by the arms and kissed him.

"Wheeew," he said and shrugged his shoulders. "That was something all right."

"I can't stay long," she said. "Miss Jane is waitin' back at the boardin' house for me. She said if I stayed too long, she'd send the law lookin' for me; and I reckon she would, too."

"I brought a blanket," he said.

"Whatever for?"

"I . . . I thought maybe . . . ah, just something to sit on," he managed.

"You mean to lie down on," she teased.

"You're making me nervous, girl."

"Have you ever been with a woman?" she asked.

"How do you mean?"

"I mean, do you have any experience?"

"You mean . . . like have I ever . . ."

"Lordy, I should've known that you ain't never been with no girl just by lookin' at you." She twisted a button on his shirt and moved 'round the tree and peeked her head and stuck out her tongue.

"Oh, I suppose you are a woman of experience," he said. "I suppose you've even been to see the elephant."

"Well, I knows up from down," she said.

"Well, I reckon I do too."

"So says you."

"Do you want me to show you?"

"I don't reckon I ought to be foolin' 'round with the like of you." She showed him her smile, and everything about her made him feel as if there were springs popping loose inside him.

"Why'd you come here, then?" he asked.

"I just thought I'd come to see what it was like."

"What?"

"Kissin' a white boy."

"Well, what's it like?"

"It's okay. Ain't nothin' special in it."

"How come we done it three times then?"

"You sure do talk a lot."

"What am I supposed to do?"

"I reckon if you don't know, I ain't goin' to be the one to tell you."

He kissed her again, and she allowed it. They wrapped up in the blanket. He felt the fine smoothness of her skin, smelled the lilac freshness of her neck and shoulders. His arms and shoulders were strong, muscled; they held her so she could hardly breath.

He lay atop her, pressing down against her. She wasn't sure. His hands crawled up the sides of her legs and over her breasts, and she could hardly breathe at all!

"You'd better stop," she whispered.

"What?"

"I'm feeling all bothered," she said.

"You're *supposed* to feel all bothered."

"I don't mean in that way. I mean I can't hardly breath with you lying on top of me and trying to squeeze the life out of me with your hands. You sure do have crazy hands."

"But you got me all stirred up, Sassy."

"Well, get yourself un-stirred, Jud Corbett."

"Girls!" he muttered as he rolled off and away from her.
She sat up, straightened her clothing and smoothed her
hair, and blew a deep breath.

"I am not a floozy," she said.

"I never said you was."

"Well, if I were to lie down with every boy that came
along and wanted to, I reckon I'd be a floozy." What a
minute ago had been her passion, now had become damp
disappointment.

"Ah, don't cry," he said, not wanting to look at her directly but able to hear, plainly, her sniffling.

"I just wanted to think that maybe you cared about me
in other ways . . . other than just wantin' to lie down on
top of me and gettin' me to do it with you."

"I thought that was what you wanted," he said.

It was true. She *had* wanted it. At least a part of her had
wanted it, and a part of her still wanted it. But . . .

"I was sort of hoping that when it happened, it wouldn't
be on some horse blanket rolling around on the prairie."

Her reasoning left him uncertain. What was wrong with
a horse blanket?

"You're a sweet boy, Jud Corbett, but you don't know
beans about what a woman feels and I can't see myself
doin' it with someone that don't know beans about how I
feel. I just can't!"

"Not even a few more kisses? I'm feeling as if I've been
horse-kicked, everything's aching so bad."

"No, not one," she said. "And if you feel so bad, you
should just jump into the creek and cool yourself off."

"Dang," he muttered, his disappointment clear.

"I better get back before Miss Jane sends the law for

me," she said, adjusting the wool cape across her shoulde even though her skin felt warm.

"I'll walk you."

"No need. I made it here on my own, I can make it bac again."

"Will you come by the store tomorrow?"

"Maybe. I'll have to do some thinkin' about it."

She felt somewhat bad about sending him off like tha without a promise or even one more kiss. But she herse was confused about how she felt toward him. She'd just a soon have the time to be by herself and figure it out.

She waited until he was gone before starting back. Tr as she might, she couldn't keep her thoughts off what ha transpired while they were wrapped up together in the hor blanket. It all kept whirling around in her head: Jud Corbe and strong arms and kisses.

Before she realized it, she was halfway through the di trict, with the tracks in sight. A figure stepped from th shadows.

"Lordy!" was all that she could manage to say. She fe as if her heart were squeezed into her throat, cutting off a her air.

"No need to be frightened, gal." The voice was whisper as murderous as the sharp blade of a knife, she thought.

The man was tall and long-limbed and wearing a fringe leather jacket and a beaver hat, and he had wrought-iro black mustaches curving around the sides of his mout When he told her there was no need for her to be frightene the mustaches rose and fell like the black wings of a rave and wasn't a raven nothin' more than ol' death showin' u as a bird? Wasn't a raven about the worst thing that coul come visit a body?

"I've got to be goin' on about my business, mister." It was all she was able to summon in the way of courage.

"Sure you do, gal," he said in that knife-blade voice. She wondered if he could slice her throat with his steel-edged words.

"What do you want with a poor child like me?"

"Just a little conversation, sis."

"Please don't hurt me, mister."

"Have you ever heard of a man named Ben Moon?"

Twenty-one

It took a full week more before he could stand on his own using a stout cottonwood branch for a crutch. Kid Joe had fashioned it himself. Ten days beyond that, and he found getting around the yard of the soddy and even going as far as the privy was getting easier. Most of the soreness in his side, he had forgotten. The leg still gave him trouble.

"I had a brother shot in both legs during the war," said Fess Foley. "They had to cut 'em both off. It was at Cold Harbor. He didn't want them to cut his legs off, but they told him it was either his legs that got buried or him. He was only seventeen. It sort of cost him his outlook on life."

"I guess that makes me lucky," said Ben Moon.

"I reckon so."

Pearl had fallen in love with him, that was plain to everyone. Kid Joe teased her about it.

"You ought not to be so quick to judge," she said. "It's easy to see that you trail him around like a gosling after its mother."

"Don't either," he said.

"You're probably hoping he'll teach you how to gunfight."

It was true. It was something he thought about day and

night: Having Ben Moon teach him how to use a pistol, how to draw it out, hold it steady, and knock the blazes out of a target.

Pearl made lemonade and served it to him out in the yard. She sat nearby and watched him drink it; and when he would drain the glass, she would go and get him more.

"Kid Joe is always talking about you," she said.

"What's he say?"

"Oh, Pa showed him the article in the *Police Gazette*. He's practically wore the words off the page with his eyes he's read it so many times. Kid Joe says you're one of the most famous frontiersmen that ever lived. Kid Joe says the *Police Gazette* has quoted notable sources as having revealed that you've killed more than a hundred men in your life."

"Closer to two hundred."

"No!"

"Might even be three. I don't know. A fellow loses count after the first hundred and fifty or so." She could see then that he was teasing. She could see it by the way his colorless eyes squinted at her in sort of a half-wink.

"Kid Joe says the *Police Gazette* calls you a border man; Kid Joe says that means that you've ridden on both sides of the law."

"Well, I reckon that's true enough."

"Which was best, Mr. Moon? Which was more romantic? To be a lawman on the frontier, or a desperado?"

She watched his face intently.

A slight curve of his lips began in the farthest corners of his mouth and ever so slowly formed a smile.

"Romantic? Now that is a way that I have never thought of my life as having been: *Romantic*."

"You must know all about adventure," said Pearl.

"That and then some, Little Sis."

She hated it that he called her Little Sis. It made h
sound like she was just a girl when what she really wante
was for him to take notice of her as a woman.

The days had turned warm and pleasant. The prair
grass was beginning to green and grow up out of th
ground, and in a few more weeks it would be as tall a
a man's knee.

His leg was stiff as hell, and he had a feeling it alway
would be; at his age, a man didn't heal so well or s
quickly. He'd have to live with it, just like he had had t
live with everything else age and memory and time ha
wrought.

"Ask Kid Joe to bring me out my pistol will you, Litt
Sis?"

Kid Joe brought it, wrapped in a burlap sack and heav
as a brick.

"Set up some of your mam's old bean cans, Kid. We'
see if this ol' piece still works." Kid Joe's grin split his fac
wide open, and his protruding front teeth revealed them
selves.

"You bet."

Kid Joe lined up the cans out back away from the sodd
because Martha ordered him to. "You two want to shoo
that gun, take it away from the house," she said. "And mak
darn sure you don't hit the cow."

Ben Moon took the Starr in one hand, leaned on the co
tonwood crutch with the other. Kid Joe watched his ever
move, and Fess Foley wandered out from where he ha
been repairing a harness to watch as well.

"First thing a man ought to do," said Ben Moon, "befor
firing his piece is to check his loads. One poor load ca
cost you." Ben Moon knocked the shells from the chamber

examined them, and replaced them in the cylinder. "They seem okay," he said.

Kid Joe watched as Ben Moon lifted the Starr in a deliberate manner that was neither slow nor fast and held it straight out at the end of his arm. It seemed like a full minute before he squeezed the trigger, and the gun banged so loud it hurt Kid Joe's ears and left them ringing.

The bean can hopped into the air like a spooked rabbit, tumbled, and landed on its side. Kid Joe went to look and saw the bullet had punched a thumb-sized hole through one side and exploded out the other, leaving sharp jagged edges of tin sticking out.

Walking the distance back to where Ben Moon stood, Kid Joe counted twenty paces. It didn't seem like that much of a shot.

"I know what you're thinking, Kid. It ain't that far. Believe me, when it's the real thing, it is."

Kid Joe watched as Ben Moon *popped* four more cans into the air. Each time he did, the horses in the corral got skittish from the noise.

"Go ahead and reload and give it a shot yourself, Kid." Ben Moon looked over at Fess, then added, "if that's all right with you."

"Sure. The Kid's been aching to shoot that big pistol of yours ever since we found you. Go ahead, Kid. Show Mr. Moon what you've got."

The barrel was still warm, and Kid Joe could feel the colorless, clear eyes of Ben Moon watching him. He dropped one of the fresh shells into the dirt, felt foolish for having done so, picked it up, wiped it off, and slid it into one of the chambers.

"It's a good idea to let your hammer rest on an empty chamber, Kid. It can save your toes from getting shot off."

Kid Joe extracted one of the shells and turned the cyl
inder until the hammer rested on an empty chamber.

"Go ahead; just point it as you would your finger an
squeeze," said Ben Moon.

Pearl watched first Ben Moon, then Kid Joe, then he
daddy fire the big pistol at the tin cans. She held her hand
over her ears and blinked every time the gun was fired. I
sounded like the crash of thunder.

Later they ate beans and fried pork and cornbread an
drank bark tea that had been cooled in the summer cellar

"I'll be leaving in the morning," said Ben Moon afte
they had finished their supper.

Pearl felt her heart break at the news. Kid Joe was dis
appointed. Martha felt relieved.

"Are you up to it?" asked Fess Foley.

"I have to return to Hays. I have some business there—
people waiting for me. At least I hope they still are."

"We'll fix a wagon up and haul you there, Mr. Moon."

"No. I'd just as soon ride. I'd appreciate your selling m
a horse if you can spare one."

"I can't spare one to sell, but you can have the loan o
one. If you don't mind, I'll send Kid Joe to ride along wit
you and he can bring the animal back after you get t
Hays."

"Much obliged."

They sat for a time, smoking pipes, out in the front yar
as had become their custom. They sat in silence and listene
to the calling back and forth of coyotes. And when the coyo
tes quit calling one another, the prairie grew lonesome i
its silence.

"Ain't my business," said Fess Foley—Kid Joe was sit
ting cross-legged on the ground next to his daddy's chair—

but are you just going to head out and not do a thing
bout the men who shot you and your companion?"

"There are more important things awaiting me," said Ben
Moon, the muscles of his face knotting along the line of
his jaw.

Fess Foley shook his head and rocked back in his chair.

"It takes some man to forget about those that nearly murdered him."

"I haven't forgotten," said Ben Moon.

Kid Joe was disappointed that Ben Moon would not seek
his revenge on his assassins. According to his daddy's *Police
Gazette,* Ben Moon was not a man to be offended in any
way lest the offender taste the lead of his blazing pistols.
But, in all honesty, Ben Moon appeared, in physical stature,
no more imposing than his own pa, Fess Foley. They both
seemed, as Kid Joe sat there looking at them smoking their
pipes and studying the nothingness of dark prairie, a pair
of kindly old gents that had seen and done everything they
were ever going to.

Pearl said, "Oh, Mama. Tomorrow he will be gone and
will miss him, our gentle but dangerous Ben Moon."

Martha replied, "Stop being so dramatic, child. I for one
will breath easier when he is gone."

"Oh, Mama. You hardly understand anything at all." And
with having said the very thing that pressed her heart with
such ache, she fled to her room behind the hung blanket
and sobbed loudly enough that Martha had to go in and
comfort her.

"Your head is filled with fantasy," she told her daughter,
"but, I can understand how that can be. Sooner or later,
every woman is taken with a man like Mr. Ben Moon."

Pearl pressed her face against her mother's soft bosom
and her tears stained wet the gingham dress.

"I'm not much on thank yous," said Ben Moon, "bu
I'm indebted to you for everything."

"No need to be," said Fess Foley. "We done for you wh.
we'd have done for anyone. Kid Joe, why not go and g
us a jug out of the cellar? We ought to at least have
farewell drink." Kid Joe brought back the whiskey jug an
set it between the two men, then wandered away from th
house.

"I think he's sorry to see you go, Mr. Moon," said Fes
Foley. "I think he came to admire you. Me, I'm just a soc
buster, not much to look up to. But you, someone with yo
reputation. Well, that's another matter."

Ben Moon winced at the suggestion.

"There're lots of things wrong in this world for a youn
man to admire," said Ben Moon. "That don't make it righ
You keep a rein on Kid Joe, teach him a trade and he'
thank you for it."

"It's hard to get wild notions out of a boy's head," sai
Fess Foley, offering Ben Moon the jug of whiskey.

He took it, drank in silence, and handed it back.

"Tell him to remember how he and you found me ou
there on the prairie shot full of holes, nearly dead. Tell hi
to remember that and not what he reads in the *Police G*
zette. Maybe it will make the difference."

"I think he will remember once you're gone. If not, I'
remind him sure enough. Kid Joe's got a good heart. He'
come around to his senses."

Since he had gotten well enough, Ben Moon had insiste
that his bed be moved out into the yard and that Kid Jo
and Pearl be moved back inside. Nobody had argued th
point.

He had been lying staring at the stars, the soothing effec
of the whiskey lulling him. He thought about Jane and wor

lered if maybe she had passed on in the time he had been
gone. It was possible. He wondered, too, about finding
Sarah in Denver. It wouldn't be difficult as long as she was
with Doc Pierce; but if Sarah had gone off by herself, he
might never locate her.

The dark countenance of Ned Bluecorn, passive in death,
floated into his mind. It didn't strike him as fair that Ned
had had to suffer the death he did; but then, there was little
f any justice on the frontier.

He dozed. Something awakened him. The press of someone standing near his bed. Instinctively, he reached for the
Starr: it was not there. Kid Joe had taken it into the house
earlier to clean it.

"It's just me, Mr. Moon."

"Pearl?"

"I had to come and see you now that everyone else is
asleep."

"What's the problem, Little Sis?" He sat up, noting the
twinge of pain in his leg.

"I don't want you to leave in the morning."

"I wish I didn't have to. You and your family have been
awfully kind to me. Saved my hide. Fed me. Even washed
me. A man doesn't forget such things."

She stood there, her long auburn hair unpinned and hanging down past her shoulders, the prairie wind touching the
edges of her cotton night dress. He waited for her to speak.

"I want."

"What is it, child?"

"I want to. . . . I want to share your bed." She lowered
her eyes and twisted one hand in the other. She was, he
thought, just a child—not more than a young woman.

"Can I ask why?" He stood and dropped a blanket over
her shoulders and stepped back. It was a matter of great

delicacy, one that he'd have to handle in a way that wouldn
make her feel either foolish or rejected.

Why? he had asked her. She wasn't sure why. Not exactl

"Please, Mr. Moon, don't make me try to explain it."

"There're lots of reasons I could give you about wh
such a thing would be wrong for you, Pearl. I could tal
about the difference in years between us or the fact my pas
is still trying to catch up with me or that I like living o
the move and wouldn't be any good at settling down—a
which makes me a bad prospect in the love department. Bu
I don't suppose that would do much good, so there's onl
one thing I can tell you that might make you understan
why I can't let you share my bed."

"What?"

"I already have a sweetheart, Pearl. The fact is, when sh
was younger, she looked an awful lot like you. You remin
me of her a great deal. You're as pretty as she is. I know
you can understand how it wouldn't be right under the cir
cumstances." *She should have guessed that a hero of th
plains would have a sweetheart somewhere waiting just fo
him. A sweetheart he had said that looked like her.* She fe
at once relieved by a desire she didn't fully understand an
embarrassed by her boldness.

"I guess I have made myself seem foolish to you," sh
said. "I am just a foolish girl like Mama said."

She reminded him of a daughter he did not know.

"I am flattered by your attention, Pearl. Any man woul
be."

She removed the blanket he had put around her shoulder
and handed it back.

"I'd best be getting back before Mama wakes up," sh
said.

"It'd be best," he told her.

In the warm comfort of her bed, his name galloped through her mind: *Ben Moon. Ben Moon. Ben Moon.* Like wild horses.

Twenty-two

The girl said her name was Sassy Sparks and she worke[d] for a woman named Jane Westlake, that Miss Jane was he[r] mistress. And yes, Miss Jane was sick with the lung feve[r]. And even though she was scared and her eyes rolled whit[e] she said she didn't know any Ben Moon. Then the shado[w] man pulled out a knife and showed her its blade and sai[d] it was sharp enough to cut through chain, and it made a[ll] the difference in the world.

Ben Moon had gone to Dodge. Lord! He had gone [to] Dodge nearly three weeks ago and hadn't come back since[.]

"If you're lying to me, girl. I will come back and cu[t] your head off. But, first, I will do other things to you. D[o] you believe me?"

He could hear her swallow. Then, he stepped back int[o] the shadows and wasn't there anymore. She wanted to fain[t] but could only manage to run.

He had to stop every hour; Kid Joe would help him o[ut] of the saddle and he would walk around trying to get th[e] numbness out of his leg and the pain out of his mind.

"Don't ever get yourself shot, Kid. It hurts like hell."

They reached Hays after dark.

"Take yourself a room, Kid," said Ben Moon, handin[g]

Kid Joe a pair of silver dollars. "In the morning, you get yourself a good breakfast before starting back. Stop and say goodbye before you leave."

"Yes, sir."

"There's a livery down the street where you can leave the horses for the night. Tell the fella there to charge their care to me. Good night."

"Good night, Mr. Moon."

Kid Joe had started to ride away when Ben Moon said, "Oh, Kid. Another thing. In this town, I'm known as Ben Avery."

"Yes, sir. I understand. Ben Avery."

"Thanks, Kid."

Kid Joe touched the brim of his sombrero and spurred the horses down the street.

Ben Moon climbed the stairs to the boarding house, one leg at a time, and then down the hallway to Jane's room. He knocked once, turned the handle, and stepped inside.

Jane held a cocked derringer, and Sassy crouched by her side.

"Hold up, darling, I've already been shot."

"Jesus, Ben! I thought . . ." She lowered the derringer and coughed.

"You expecting somebody?"

She told him the story about the shadow man Sassy had encountered the night before.

"Stepped out of the dark like Beezelbub himself. Scared me so bad I nearly wet my bloomers. Held a knife up and said he'd cut off my head if I was lying to him about where you was at. I wasn't about to lie for you, Ben Moon. You or that ol' ugly Indun, Ned Bluecorn. *No, sir!* That man

was a cold killer. Come out of the dark and went back i
it just like he was part of it hisself!"

He asked her soft questions about the man, but she ha
no answers. "Darkness is what he was. Death! What mor
is there to know about such a thing?"

He found a chair next to the bed. A silver flask of whis
key the doctor had said would do her no harm in taking
and might even help, stood within reach.

"Do you mind?" he asked.

"No. Did you say you were shot? And where is Ned?"

He unscrewed the cap to the flask, held the thin meta
bottle in his hand for a moment, and then tipped it to hi
lips, hoping the fire would burn out the pain.

"We were ambushed outside of Dodge. Ned was killed.

Jane uttered a single word. "No."

"Some men came by the next day and found me. If the
hadn't come along, Ned and I would both be planted unde
the prairie."

Sassy could not imagine the big Indian as having bee
murdered. Her fear increased. If Ned Bluecorn could b
murdered, any one of them could be murdered; and she ha
nearly been so. *Lord Jesus!*

"Sarah?" asked Jane. "Did you locate Sarah?"

The whiskey ran through his veins like a brush fire. H
grew tired all at once.

"No, not exactly. But, I know where she is, where she
gone."

"Tell me where?"

"To Denver with a man named Doc Pierce." He went o
to tell her about the fate of the Schultzmans. He could se
the news tug at the corners of her mouth. He waited fo
her to cry or say something; she did neither.

"Will we ever be able to find her, Ben? Our Sarah?"

"Doc Pierce is well known wherever he travels," said Ben Moon, tipping the flask once more to his lips. "If I can find Doc Pierce, I stand a good chance of finding Sarah."

They sat, the three of them, in a circle of silence for a time, the tick of the Regulator clock their heartbeat.

"You look terrible, Ben. Why not get some rest? You've done all that you can do for now. Poor Ned. He died for nothing."

He stood slowly, pulling the bad leg up behind him, and limped to the door.

"Ned was a good man," he said, then turned and closed the door behind him.

Sassy said, "I can't hardly believe Ned Bluecorn is dead."

He was already sitting on the porch of the Hays House, smoking a cigarette and sipping a cup of coffee, when Kid Joe rode up the following morning.

"Well, Kid, how'd you sleep?"

"Fine, Mr. Moon."

"You tell you're daddy when you get back home that I appreciate everything."

"I will." Kid Joe touched his heels to his mount.

"Oh, and Kid?"

Kid Joe turned the horse around.

"Do you reckon your daddy would mind your having this old Starr of mine?"

Kid Joe's eyes grew as big as tea saucers.

"I couldn't take your piece, Mr. Moon. What would you have to fight with?"

"I don't intend on getting in any more fights, Kid."

He pulled the Starr from his coat pocket and held it out to the boy.

Kid Joe leaned from his saddle, stared at the gun, and

then shoved it into his belt. There were a lot of words
his mouth he wanted to speak, to tell Ben Moon, but no
of them seemed to want to come out.

"You ride carefully, Kid. Tell your ma and Pearl I sa
thanks as well. Especially them."

Kid Joe nodded and tugged the brim of his hat dov
lower and put his horse into a trot.

Ben had already made up his mind. As soon as he f
ished his coffee, he would walk over to the train stati
and buy a ticket for Denver. A hot bath, a shave, and so
fresh clothes might not hurt, either.

Sam Pepper reached Dodge at noon. He had heard
mors that Billy Tibbs was marshalling the town; that seem
like some sort of joke, because Billy Tibbs used to r
stolen cattle and horses between the Texas Panhandle a
Silver City in New Mexico. And, at one time, there b
even been strong talk about Billy Tibbs being a road age
whose specialty was the Bisbee to Tombstone stage line

He found Billy along with three deputies in the Bu
Head Saloon. Billy was wearing big Mexican spurs and
cowhide vest with a badge pinned to it. He wore a pair
pistols in a cross-draw.

The deputies all wore badges, too, and had the bla
stares of humorless men. *That was Billy, always actı
tougher than he was, always surrounding himself with b
characters.*

Sam Pepper ordered whiskey in full view of the lawm
and waited for Billy to acknowledge his presence, but
acknowledgment was forthcoming.

"Maybe it's because I started dressing better, Bill."

"What?" Billy Tibbs looked up for the first time; all three deputies looked up, too.

"Maybe that's why you didn't recognize me—because of my clothes."

Billy looked hard with his close-set eyes, his thick brows furrowing into a ridge of shaggy hair.

"Do I know you?"

"You once did."

"I don't recall, mister."

"Sam Pepper, Bill. Do you recall me now?"

He saw some of the menace drop away from the square face of the lawman; he saw the three deputies exchange looks.

"What are you doing in Dodge, Pepper?"

"I'm looking for somebody. Somebody we both knew a time back. Before we all took up honest professions." The sarcasm seemed to be lost on the lawman.

"Who might that be?"

"Ben Moon."

Billy Tibbs snorted, looked around at his deputies then back at Sam Pepper.

"What you looking for Ben Moon for?"

"That's a private matter."

A slow grin spread across the fleshy lips of the lawman.

"If you've got any business with Ben Moon, you're too late."

"How so?"

" 'Cause I killed him three weeks ago."

"You, Billy?"

"Are you saying I didn't?" He saw the deputies stiffen: it was obvious that the liquor he had been drinking was the spark behind his sudden belligerence.

"These boys help you, did they?"

"Yeah. They was in on it. Ben Moon came riding in kickir
up a fuss about this that and the other thing. I ordered hi:
to leave town. And when he wouldn't. I arrested him. F
broke jail, killed one of my best men. I went after him wi
these boys, and we hunted him down and killed him out c
the prairie; and that's where he's at now, if you want him."

It was one hell of a story if it were true, but it didr
figure.

"Well, I guess I *am* too late," said Sam Pepper. "Let n
buy you and these boys a round and say congratulation
Ridding the territory of Ben Moon is quite a feat. I h:
intended on doing it myself, but it looks as though you hav
beaten me to it."

It was flattering talk coming from a man like Sam Peppe
The kind of talk that Billy Tibbs welcomed, for he kne
Sam Pepper to be a killer and fearless. Billy Tibbs had r
wish for gunplay with a man like Sam Pepper.

They drank amicably for several hours, and Sam Pepp•
had Billy Tibbs talk about the gun battle between himse
and his deputies and Ben Moon. *How exactly had it ha*
pened?

Billy delighted in telling and re-telling the story, eac
time embellishing it further, changing it in its detail; th
ample supply of liquor that the infamous Sam Pepper w:
buying him made Billy Tibbs's tongue wag around in h
mouth like a pair of long drawers drying in a stiff wind.

In one of the tellings, it came out that Ben Moon h:
been in town looking for Doc Pierce. He hadn't said wh
but that Doc had left with a gal for Denver shortly befo•
Ben Moon arrived.

"Too damn bad that he ain't never going to find whatev
it was he was looking for. Doc's an old friend of mine,

reckon I did him a favor as well," chortled the drunken lawman.

"Where exactly did the killing take place, Billy?"

"What the hell difference does it make?"

"I'd just like to see it for myself is all. No particular reason."

"Hell, I'm about ready to fall into a hole," said Billy.

"Come on, Billy, tell me exactly where it was you killed ol' Ben Moon. It's something I just have to see for myself." The request was said with a steady, unflinching stare—one that delivered its meaning even through the haze of drunkenness.

"I'll have one of the boys take you out there tomorrow so's you can see. Right now, I'm as drunk as a coon and need to lay my head down or I might not live to see another day."

The next day, two of the steel-eyed deputies rode him out to the spot where the killing had occurred. There was a single plot of disturbed sod that indicated a recent grave.

"Is this it?" asked Sam Pepper. He could see the look of confusion on their faces; something was wrong.

The two deputies watched, smoking cigarettes as Sam Pepper dug the spade he had brought along into the soft, partly sunken patch of ground.

"Somebody must have buried them both in the same grave," muttered one of the lawmen. The other nodded.

It was work that caused a sweat, grave digging. But he did it with intent, for if Billy Tibbs had told the truth, was five hundred dollars worth of man lying in the grave.

It didn't take long for the shovel to strike something that

wasn't sod. Sam Pepper took caution and used his hands
to pull up the upper torso of the corpse.

He studied it for a full minute and then released it back
to its resting place.

"You gents care to tell me how this Indian got into Ben
Moon's grave?" Sam Pepper demanded, brushing dirt from
his clothes.

The two men exchanged looks and hunched their shoul
ders.

"He was with Ben Moon the night we . . ."

"The night you ambushed them," said Sam Pepper. "Tha
man's still wrapped up in his blanket, and the blanket is
full of bullet holes."

"It was Billy that ordered it," said the other deputy. He
had long silvery mustaches and honest blue eyes. "Jip here
will confirm, won't you, Jip? Me, I'm tired to hell of tha
lying sonofabitch, Billy Tibbs."

"Well, you boys had better go back and tell Billy tha
the only thing he killed was an Indian in his sleep. That's
a damn far sight from killing Ben Moon. Tell Billy, if I
were him, I'd be concerned."

Sam Pepper sat on the hump of fresh dug soil and gave
a laugh as the two men rode back toward Dodge.

"I guess that it's meant that you be killed by a true pro
fessional, Ben Moon, and not some low-life drunken law
man. God forbid any of us have to die that way."

Twenty-three

Wyatt Tibidoux was a short, solidly built man with close-cropped iron-gray hair and brackish eyes. He had been chief of police of Denver for nearly five full years. He had thirty policemen on staff, and he prided himself in the toughness of his department.

Wyatt Tibidoux's hands were a mark of his character. They were scarred, thick and meaty, each with a bank of ridged knuckles that could break a jaw and lay their victim low. He didn't mind beating an offender into submission, had in fact earned a reputation as a fighter. He wore no pistols.

Wyatt Tibidoux sat in his office rubbing the scarred knuckles of one hand, rubbing at the arthritic ache that age had brought.

Before him on his desk were the twin, filigreed frames that contained tintypes of a woman and a small girl. They each had dark hair and curls. The child looked much like the woman. He had lost them both to typhoid two years before. He never looked at the images without having to close his eyes and choke back a memory. The memory was always different but somehow the same.

The door to his office opened suddenly, admitting a bright shaft of light. Standing within the light was a tall man.

Wyatt Tibidoux released the hand he been rubbing and placed it atop his desk. The figure in the light remained

there a moment longer before stepping fully inside and clos
ing the door behind him.

The light was bad in the room, dim. The man move
with a limp.

"Is there something I can do for you?" Tibidoux's voic
was deep, coming from his broad chest, just the way Be
Moon remembered it.

"Wyatt," said the man, removing his hat and rubbing
sleeve across his brow.

The man's stance seemed vaguely familiar—the way h
moved; the way he held his hat. But, Wyatt Tibidoux didn
know this man.

"You've got me, mister. Do we know each other?"

"I know it's been a few years, Wyatt, but have I change
all that much?"

Wyatt Tibidoux's eyes narrowed; his own damn vanit
would not allow him to wear the spectacles he carried i
his vest pocket. His brow furrowed as he examined the ma
standing before him.

He shook his head. "I can't place you."

"Ben Moon, Wyatt."

"Ben Moon? Hell, that's a laugh. Ben Moon was kille
in El Paso five, maybe six, years ago."

"It's me, Wyatt."

Wyatt Tibidoux's disbelieving expression did not change

"No. It can't be. I knew Ben Moon, and you ain't him."

"You had a sister named Laura Lee and a brother name
Tom."

Wyatt Tibidoux stood with deliberation; his chair scrape
across the floor. He leaned for a closer look.

"Damned if it *ain't* you!" *What had become of the Be
Moon he had known? This man was gaunt and used up. Ola*

"Damned if it ain't."

Slowly the meaty hand of Wyatt Tibidoux extended itself and Ben Moon shook it, noting its strength.

"Did you fall off your horse?" the lawman asked, acknowledging the limp he had noted earlier.

"No."

"It's hard to believe," said Wyatt Tibidoux. "It's like seeing someone that's come back from the dead."

"It sort of feels like that at times, Wyatt. How are your wife and daughter?"

The lawman's square features receded into the dark furrowed creases of a face that had grieved much.

"Lost them both. Life ain't been the same for me since."

"Would you drink a whiskey with me, Wyatt?"

"I've lost my taste for it, Ben. Just as I've lost my taste for everything except upholding the law."

"I'm sorry things have gone that way for you, Wyatt."

"Don't be."

"You have come far from the days when we used to drive cows down along the Brazos. Chief of police here in Denver. You've done better than most of us."

"You've come here for a reason, Ben. I've never known you to go anywhere without a reason."

"I have."

"Tell me about it."

"I've come to find someone, a girl . . . a young woman."

"Denver's a big town."

"She's with Doc Pierce."

Chief Tibidoux grunted as though something were troubling his digestion.

"Talk has it that Doc's in town. He's been spotted from time to time in a couple of the gambling dens."

Ben Moon said, "Do you mind if I sit a spell? I've come a long way."

"Do you mean to kill Doc when you catch up to him?"

"I told you, I'm looking for a young woman that's traveling with him. That's the whole of it."

"I won't tolerate any assassinations in my town. Not from you, not from anybody."

"You don't have to worry. Hell, I even gave some kid my pistol before I came out here. What's that tell you?"

"Tells me you're either a damn fool or you've found Jesus."

"Neither."

"Sit a spell and catch me up on past times. Much as I hate to admit it, I still miss the old days."

They talked about who was left, about who wasn't. They talked about the way it was and about how it had become.

There was Stubby Patterson, who was murdered by a pimp in Waco. And July Bird, who drowned crossing the Canadian trying to save one stupid cow. There was Dandy Bill, who simply died of cancer, and Little Bob Spencer who blew his brains out.

"Jane's dying," Ben Moon said.

"Jane? Jane from Kansas?"

Ben Moon nodded his head and made a cigarette and smoked it.

"You and she were sweethearts as I recall," said Wyatt Tibidoux.

"Nearly married," said Ben Moon. "I should've asked her; now it's too late."

"There's nothing like a good woman," said the police man.

"No, I reckon not."

Tibidoux remembered the woman in the picture frame remembered her sweet laughter, her soft warmth.

"Jane's why I'm here, Wyatt."

"How so?"

"It's her daughter, the young woman that I'm looking for."

"The one with Doc?"

Ben Moon nodded, stubbed the cigarette under the heel of his boot, blew out the last of the blue smoke.

He explained; the policeman listened.

"Jane's in Hays right now, waiting for me. She doesn't have long, Wyatt. Even if I can find the girl here in Denver, it may be too late."

"Well, Ben, Denver's a grown-up town with lots of places to be lost in. But if Doc is here, we ought at least to be able to find him. Doc's has a reputation with the ladies and he cards. I can send a man to help you find him, if you want."

"I'd appreciate it, Wyatt. Are you sure you won't change your mind about the whiskey?"

"Whiskey and horses are hard on men our age, Ben. I've suffered my share of hard times. I read the Bible now and practice the law. Outside of that, I sleep good at nights. That's about all I can hope for."

"Can you recommend a place to stay? Something quiet."

Chief of Police Wyatt Tibidoux recommended a boarding house on the west side of town. "It's run by a woman with several small children. She'd be a prize to catch if it weren't for all the little ones she has running around. It'd try a man's spirits, that many kids."

They shook hands, and the policeman watched Ben Moon walk down the street with that limp that seemed to take all the effort he had. He looked for all the world like an old veteran instead of who he was: Ben Moon!

Take care ol' cuss, take care.

Ben found the boarding house and the woman who ran

it and all of her children. She wasn't quite the catch tha
Wyatt Tibidoux had described, but she was cheery an
pleasant and had cheeks as red as apples and one room lef
he could board in.

The house smelled of baking bread, and the room sh
led him into was as pleasant as she was. It had plenty o
light from a tall window with chintz curtains and a be
long enough to let him lie comfortably.

"Six bits—that includes supper," she said. "Do you lik
it?"

He noticed her looking at his leg. "Fell off my horse,"
he said.

"Oh. Horses scare me so." Three youngsters clung to he
skirts the whole time. They stared at him with round curiou
eyes and sucked their thumbs. "These are some of my ba
bies," she said proudly. "I've six. Do you have any children
mister . . ."

"Avery," he said. "Name's Ben Avery."

"Do you have any children, Mr. Avery?"

"Yes, ma'am. I have a daughter." It sounded strange t
him, sounded like a lie, but it wasn't.

"Well, then, you know what a caution kids can be." Sh
smiled and patted one of the little ones on the head. "Sup
per's at five sharp in the dining room if you care to joi
us." He watched as she headed down the hall, the thre
youngsters trailing after her like ducklings.

The conductor announced, "Denver Station," and San
Pepper came out of a drowse. He looked out the window
of the passenger car and saw the gaslights of the city. H
had come full circle since having received the letter fron

Mrs. Duvall. Hell, if he'd known, he could have just stayed out and let ol' Ben Moon come to him.

He departed the train and went directly to his room at the Marsden House, a big square two-story brick building that stood on the corner of Colfax and Second Streets.

He dropped his pistols on the bed and sat in a chair near the window. Somewhere down on those streets, he thought, was Ben Moon. Trouble was, he'd have to find Doc Pierce and the girl traveling with him first. Find them, and eventually find Ben Moon.

What had started out as a simple task had grown in its difficulty.

He changed clothes and re-armed himself. There was no need to waste any time. He'd have to be slick about it. Wyatt Tibidoux bossed the law in town, and Wyatt Tibidoux had once been saddle partners with Ben Moon.

If he were to kill Ben Moon in Wyatt Tibidoux's town, he'd have to damn sure do it in a way that no one would know.

He descended the stairs and went through the lobby and out onto Colfax Street. A trolley clanged past and then several carriages. *Where to begin?*

Twenty-four

"Do you like Denver?" he asked.

"I miss Kansas," she said.

"That wasn't the question."

"There's a difference."

"Of course. But how do you find it, Denver?"

"It seems full of tragedy. I miss Kansas."

"Kansas. How could anybody miss Kansas? It's still the wild frontier."

"It's where I grew up."

"Nothing but wind and grass. Cowboys!"

"You don't understand, Doc."

"I do."

"Denver depresses me."

"You'll grow used to it."

"No."

"We won't stay forever, then," he said. "We'll move on San Francisco, maybe. I'll earn us a stake at the tables, and we will go to San Francisco. You'll like San Francisco."

"It will just take me farther away."

"From what?"

"My home."

"Sarah, there is nothing left back there for you. Your family is gone. There's nothing there but that big empty house. The one you couldn't wait to leave, remember?"

She saw it now—the house. Mama and Papa's house, and ers. She remembered summers of grasshoppers in the yard nd glowbugs at night. She remembered winters with snow-rifts up to the windows and the rows of crystal-clear icicles anging from the roof. She remembered a black-and-white og and plenty of cats.

She remembered a pony. *Whatever happened to the pony?*

Doc had misled her; she had misled herself. She couldn't lame Doc.

Doc had been a dream, a fantasy. He had come at the ight time, had pronounced himself a knight in shinning rmor—she, the heroine that needed saving from the lonely astle.

Doc had wooed her, but she had allowed it, had encour-ged it. It had all been too fast, a fire upon the prairie lown by the hot winds of her own passion. *Or was it passion at all?*

Had it really only been a month ago when Doc had ridden nto her life? It seemed she had known Doc forever, that he had never not known him.

Doc was handsome. As handsome as any man she had ver seen. *But was that enough for her?*

"Maybe we should marry, Sarah."

"What?"

Doc had a habit of pacing a room.

"I said, maybe we ought to get married. You know I care or you."

"I should be flattered," she said.

"But you're not."

"It's not that I'm not, Doc."

"What is it, then?"

"I just don't think we should be married."

"Why?"

"Because I don't love you, for one thing."

"You could learn."

"How? How can you learn to love someone if you don' already?"

"Folks do it all the time."

"I can't."

Doc's handsome face took on a gloominess as he paced

"I don't understand."

"I can't explain it beyond that," she said. '

At first, Doc and everything about him had been exciting He had taken her to the opera and Delmonico's and to the zoo. At the opera, the diva's voice had made her weep and Doc had offered his handkerchief to dry her tears. And later Doc had taken her to a great ballroom and they had danced an entire evening to the music of a live band and drunk champagne and afterwards walked home instead of taking a cab

No one could be as charming as Doc when he tried.

She did not understand why she had not fallen in love with Doc. There was a great emptiness in her that she could not explain to Doc or to herself. It was more than just being homesick. But what exactly, she could not say.

"Will you stay with me awhile longer?" he asked.

"Perhaps, but not very long," she said.

"Just awhile longer then."

"Yes," she agreed.

Later, Doc had gone out alone as he had done often in the last weeks. Doc was by nature a restless soul. He could never just sit and talk. He had to be busy, and what he most kept himself busy with was his gambling. She sat quietly in her room by the window and watched and listened to the traffic in the streets below. Denver seemed another world to her.

Doc found his pleasure in such places as J&R's Gentle

men's Club, Nel's Rusty Nugget, and Diamond Jim's Long-horn Saloon.

This particular night, Doc Pierce found his way to Hattie's Old Time Saloon on the city's north side. He had heard a particularly big game was being put together. It was one he wanted in on.

"Doc," said the proprietress, Hattie Lumbager, a big German woman who outweighed most of her clientele.

"Hattie," he said. "I understand a game is being put together for the night?"

"A very big game, Doc."

"Is there a chance I can sit in?"

"A man with your reputation, Doc, I don't see how they can refuse you."

She led him to one of the tables where several men sat, their coats removed, their sleeves rolled up.

"Gents," announced Hattie. "This here is Doc Pierce and he would like to play cards with you." They all gave Doc their attention, and one said, "This is high-stakes poker, sir."

Doc patted his vest pocket.

"I had hoped it was."

"Sharps and bottom dealers ain't welcome," said another.

Doc gave him the eye and said, "I don't have to cheat, mister."

They played several hands, and Doc lost each time. He learned through the course of their conversation that two of the men were bankers; the third, a lawyer; and the fourth man, a man named Clemens, was a mine owner.

The mine owner, Clemens, seemed the most skillful of the lot. He played a wide-open brand of cards and drank his whiskey straight up and clean. He was a big, blustery fellow with thick white hair and ice-blue eyes that the whiskey had reddened.

"I've heard of you, Pierce," he said at one point. "You're supposed to be something special with the paste boards—and the ladies!" His rolling thunder laugh filled the room.

"No, nothing special," said Doc. The mine owner's gaze came to rest on Doc, came to rest in a manner that spoke of some personal irritation over the presence of Doc Pierce.

"You're acting awful humble for a man with your reputation," said Clemens. There was no kindness in his words. Doc allowed the conversation between them to drop.

Doc's mind was on Sarah. He was careless in the cards he threw away, the ones he held on to. He excused himself from the table and sought out Hattie Lumbager. She was with two miners who were busy trying to stuff money into the cleavage of her breasts.

"What's the trouble, Doc?"

"It's not going so well," he said.

"They're big-time players," she said. "I wouldn't let losing to men like that trouble you."

"It ain't that, Hattie. I've played with plenty of men better than those fellows."

"Do you want a drink?" she asked.

"Something stronger," he said.

"Are you sure, Doc?"

"I'm sure."

"In the back, last door on the left. China Charley's in the back. He'll take care of you."

Doc nodded and went to the rear of the bar and beyond a curtain. He passed down a long hall with doors on either side. The doors led to the cribs where Hattie's girls did their business.

He reached the last door on the left and knocked.

"Come in. Come in." The voice was distinctly Oriental.

The room was dimly lit by a dozen or so candles. There was no furniture in the room except for several straw mats.

"You want opium, you pay first," said the Celestial.

"How much?" asked Doc.

"One dollar," said the man. His skin was as yellow as candle wax.

Doc dropped a standing liberty silver dollar into the man's hand.

"You take off boots and go over there," the man said, pointing to one of the straw mats. "China Charley fix you up quick."

He sat on the mat and waited while the old man fixed the pipe.

"Best to lay back and enjoy it, mista."

He had forgotten how seductive the opium was. He lost himself in it; time and present awareness slipped away into the clouded air of the room. The Chinese squatted beside him.

"Tell me the future, China Charley," he said, barely able to lift his eyelids to gaze on the old man's face.

"Sure, sure. China Charley tell you everything."

The old man talked, but many of the words were lost in the blue fog of Doc's mind.

"Good fortune find you, mista," he kept hearing the old man say. "Good fortune for you."

"When?"

"Soon. Very, very soon. You see."

Doc sucked on the pipe and let the sweetness of the smoke invade his lungs. He leaned back upon the mat. It was so very very pleasant.

"You see," he could hear the Chinese say from what seemed a long way off.

"What, Charley? What am I supposed to see?"

"You see, you have very good fortune. Even tonight Charley no lie."

The old man saw Doc smile, and he in turn smiled. A smile much like that of a serpent.

Doc waited while the opium did its work. And when it had, he lifted himself dreamily from the mat, pulled on his boots, and left the room.

He passed the table where Hattie sat; a drunken miner's head rested on her bosom.

"How are you set, Doc?"

"Fine," he said.

"Be careful, Doc."

He waited until a place opened at the table, then sat back in. The lawyer had dropped out, and a man with sandy mustaches had taken his place.

Clemens said to the new man, "This here is the great Doc Pierce. I suppose you've heard of him?" The man with the mustaches said he hadn't.

Doc knew it was an effort on Clemens' part to goad him. But his mind had been calmed by the visit to China Charley's and all he wanted to do now was play poker. He bough in.

Just how long had passed, Doc could only guess, but his luck had turned, just as China Charley predicted it would. *Good fortune soon.* Isn't that what China Charley had said?

With each pot that Doc raked in, the mine owner, Clemens, became more abusive in his language towards Doc But somehow it didn't matter. All that mattered was winning.

Another hour passed and the pots increased, for Clemens insisted that the limits be taken off. Doc agreed. One o

he bankers dropped out. That left the other banker, the man
vith the sandy mustaches, Clemens, and Doc.

A crowd collected. A crowd of faces in the shadows
naintaining a vigilance over the poker players.

The pot grew to nearly a thousand dollars. The other
anker folded. The man with the sandy mustaches called,
hen raised the bet two hundred more. Clemens threw in
he last of his pile. Doc raised. Clemens was drunk and
elligerent and took umbrage at Doc's playing habits.

"You are a son of a bitch!"

Doc blinked at the insult.

His hands seemed slow, like the rest of him. He was still
eaching for his pistol when the man with the sandy mus-
aches shot him.

"Kill the cheating bastard, Bob!" shouted Clemens. Doc
elt the floor slam into him. He tasted dirty sawdust in his
nouth.

"Someone's killed Doc Pierce!" he heard someone shout.
Could it be true?

He heard Hattie Lumbager say, "Jezzus Christ, what have
ou fellows done?"

"We have seen the last of Doc Pierce," Clemens an-
ounced. "My brother Bob caught him cheating!"

"Look!" someone said. "His eyes are still open!"

China Charley came and squatted before him, the yellow
erpent smile inches from his face.

"I thought you said good fortune," whispered Doc.

"Soon," said the Oriental. "Very, very soon."

Doc didn't understand. He felt the last of his life ebb
way.

Twenty-five

"I have found your man," Wyatt Tibidoux announced.

"Pierce?"

"Yes."

"Where is he?"

"Densmore's Funeral Parlor."

"Dead?"

"Shot just this night in a gambling game."

Ben Moon pulled out the nickel pocket watch and looked at the time. It was nearly five in the morning. Not yet light outside.

"Hell!"

"Do you want to go over and have a look at him?"

"Are you sure it's Doc?"

"Yeah, it's Doc. He's still a handsome man, even in death."

"Was there a woman with him at the time?"

"Witnesses said no. Said he was alone."

"When's the burying?"

"Today, I reckon. Noon, maybe. It's the preferred time."

"Wyatt?"

"Yeah, Ben?"

"Any word on where Doc had been staying before he got killed?"

"The Denver Hotel. You reckon that's where the girl's at?"

"Maybe so."

"You want me to go along?"

"No. It's not necessary. Thanks for letting me know."

"I reckon you'll be leaving the city soon."

"Soon enough, Wyatt."

"That's good, Ben. Men like you and Doc just bring trouble. Nothing personal. It's just that I don't need more trouble than what's already here."

"I understand, Wyatt. You take care."

Wyatt Tibidoux nodded and closed the door behind him.

When she opened the door to the knocking, a tall, gaunt man stood in its framework.

"Are you Sarah?" he asked. "Sarah Schultzman?"

"I am."

"I have news for you."

"Have we met somewhere before?" she asked.

"No. Never."

"I'm afraid I wouldn't feel comfortable asking you into my room."

"Doc Pierce is dead," he said. "Shot over a card game a few hours ago."

She brought her hand to her mouth but did not say anything.

"There is more," he said.

She stared into the clear, colorless eyes.

"Did you know Doc?" she asked.

"No. Not really."

"Were you with him at the time?"

"No. I was told about it."

"How did you know about me?"

"That is why I'm here."

She saw something in the colorless eyes that appealed t
her trust.

"Come in."

She was prettier than the picture Jane had shown hin
For one thing, she was tall, like him. But she had all c
Jane's younger beauty.

"Did you hurt yourself?" she asked, noticing his limp.

"An accident," he said.

She offered him one of the horsehair chairs. He sat, keep
ing his leg out straight.

There was an awkward moment of silence.

"May I ask your name?" she asked.

"Ben Moon."

"It seems to fit you, the name Ben."

He reached inside his coat pocket and took out the letter
that Jane had given him. The packet was tied with a blu
ribbon. He held them out to her.

"If you read these, you will better understand why I ar
here," he said.

"This is all so mysterious."

He stared at the flocked wallpaper of the room while sh
read the letters. Occasionally, he allowed himself to star
at her. It seemed strange that there sat his only living kir
his daughter.

When she finished the last letter, she looked up, her eye
filled with tears.

"Am I to understand that this woman, this Jane Westlake
is my true mother?"

"She is."

He saw the tears spilling down her cheeks and instinc
tively he reached out and touched a hand to her face. "Eas
child. I know it must be a shock to you."

She recoiled slightly from his touch. Biting her lower lij

e said, "My true mother is dead, buried in Kansas. This
oman is not my true mother."

"Well, I can see how you'd want to believe that after all
is time. You've every right. But there is something you
ed to know."

"Who are you to her?" Sarah demanded.

"Just a friend," he said. "An old friend."

"She must be heartless to have sent you. Why else would
e have you carry such upsetting news as this?"

"She's dying, Sarah. She's dying fast. She wants to see
ou before she goes."

"You've wasted your time, Mr. Moon. My family is al-
ady dead."

"No. No they're not," he said. "Maybe the family that
ised you day to day and cared for you and loved you and
pt you under their roof. But, Jane's your family, too. She
nt money every month, just as is indicated in those letters,
d she never spent a day that she didn't think about you
d fret over your well-being."

"It doesn't make her my mother, that she did those things.
what these letters say are true, she gave me up when I
as born. She didn't bother to even try and raise me. What
rt of mother would do that, Mr. Moon?"

"You're full of anger and grief, girl. And I'd say give it
me time to settle in, but there's no time left. Not for her
ere ain't. Let me take you to see her. What can it cost
ou to go to a dying woman?"

She stared at the stack of letters, stared at the words, the
ursive scrawl in faded black ink. They had been written
the loving simplistic hand of her mother, Hanna. They
d praised the woman, Jane, for her kindness and gener-
ity.

She picked up one she had set aside and reread a line

from the third paragraph: *I know how much you must lo*
and miss our dear sweet Sarah. She has been our treasu
throughout the years. What a gift you have given us. If on
you could come to know her as we have . . .

She wept bitterness and sorrow and regret. Her pa
turned into his own as he watched her bury her face in h
hands and suffer the emotion of the news he had carri
to her. He could only watch. It was the most joyless thi
he had ever done.

After what seemed a long time, she lifted her face to hi

"I will go with you to see her," she said.

"I'm glad you could see your way to do it," he told h

"Will you afford me some privacy in order to get rea
for the journey?"

"I'll go and buy us tickets on the train."

"I will wait here for you."

With great effort, he stood, settling the injured leg und
him before trying to take his leave.

"You must love her a great deal," she said.

"What makes you think so?"

"When you talk about her, your eyes fill up with light

He settled his hat on his head and rolled the brim ju
so in his hands and then gave it all a slight tug.

"Well, I guess I'd be lying to you to deny it."

They stayed that way for a long full moment, lookin
into one another's eyes, understanding what the other wa
feeling, understanding pain and loss and longing. He kne
in that instant what it felt like to be a father and it caus
him to swallow down the feeling lest he tell her the rest
the truth. He figured she had enough to deal with the wa
it was.

* * *

The article in that morning's edition of the Denver *Post* read: THE WELL KNOWN AND MOST RECENT RESIDENT OF THIS CITY, GAMBLER DOC PIERCE, WAS SHOT DEAD IN ONE OF THE MORE NOTORIOUS LOCAL ESTABLISHMENTS, HATTIE'S SALOON, OVER A POKER GAME. ANOTHER KILLING HAS TAKEN PLACE IN OUR TOWN. THE VIOLENCE CONTINUES. WITNESSES SAID HE WAS SHOT IN SELF-DEFENSE. THE MAN WHO DID THE SHOOTING WAS NOT READILY IDENTIFIED. SEVERAL HUNDRED DOLLARS WAS AT STAKE. THE BURIAL WILL TAKE PLACE AT NOON TODAY IN THE OLD CITY CEMETERY SOUTH OF TOWN. MR. PIERCE'S REMAINS ARE ON DISPLAY AT DENSMORE'S FUNERAL PARLOR.

Sam Pepper folded the paper and laid it on the table over his plate of half-eaten eggs. *Bad news.* He placed a dollar on the table and took his leave.

"Yes, sir. May I help you?" The man who greeted him at the door of the mortuary had a whispery voice and cavernous eyes.

"I came to visit Doc Pierce, or what's left of him."

"Yes, sir, right this way."

Sam Pepper was led into a room that was cool and dim. There were heavy purple-velvet drapes on the windows, and the room had the sickly sweet odor of rotting flowers.

The man lifted the lid of a pine coffin that rested on a pair of saw horses.

"Was he a friend, sir?"

"No, but he could've been if he had lived long enough."

"Indeed, sir. He was a well-known character of the West."

"So I heard."

"Seems peaceful, does he not?"

"Yep, like he's asleep."

"Eternal rest."

"Tell me something. Has anybody come to visit oth‹ than me? A woman, maybe?"

"Yes. There was a young woman earlier. Quite prett‹ She was with a gentleman. A somewhat . . . ah, desperat‹ looking man. Tall. Much older than she."

"Did this fellow have eyes that looked like clear glass?

"Yes. It was his eyes that I remember most about hir Most unusual in coloration, or shall I say lack of. In n‹ profession one takes care to notice such things."

"How long ago were they here?"

"Oh, about an hour, maybe less. The man said somethir to the young lady about their need to catch a train. The‹ did not stay long."

"You can put the lid back on," said Sam Pepper.

"Would you care to purchase a photograph of the d‹ ceased, sir? I had several made up as mementos."

The man produced one of the photographs and hand‹ it to Sam Pepper. It showed the reposed visage of Dc Pierce, his hair neatly combed and his skin as white ‹ flour.

"Very good likeness, wouldn't you say?"

"Looks like every other dead man I've seen," said Sa‹ Pepper handing back the photograph.

"Only a dollar each," said the mortician.

"No thanks, friend."

He made his way to the train station and stood in li‹ behind two women with gray hair and large bustles. Whe the women had finished purchasing their tickets to Tell‹ ride, he stepped to the counter. The clerk eyed him throug smudged spectacles.

"Did a man and a young woman purchase tickets here
earlier?"

"Lots of folks purchased tickets earlier."

"This man had clear eyes, the kind you wouldn't forget."

The clerk touched a mole high on his cheek, squinted
both eyes for a second, then remembered. "Yep. Seen a man
like that. Bought two tickets to Hays, Kansas, on the Morning Flyer. Left thirty minutes ago. Right on time as usual."

"When's the next one go?"

"Same time tomorrow, same time every day except Sundays."

Killing Ben Moon was going to be easy. It was catching
up with him that was proving to be a damn chore.

"How much for a ticket?"

"Sixteen dollars and twenty-five cents."

He'd have to remember to add it to his expense account.

Twenty-six

She proved a quiet girl with inquisitive eyes as the train rolled across the flat plains of eastern Colorado and, through the night, onto the flat plains of Kansas that were just now coming alive in new prairie grass.

He didn't know what to say to her. She did not bother to ask much of him.

He stepped out onto the platform of the car and smoked a cigarette; they'd be in Hays within the hour. He was glad it was over.

The wheels clacked against the steel rails and the wind rushed past and it seemed like it had been a long time since Ned Bluecorn had ridden out to the shack that morning when he first heard the ice breaking up on the river.

She stepped out onto the platform next to him, the wind pushing at her bonnet. He noticed how truly pretty she was.

"Tell me about her," she said. "Tell me about Jane."

"What would you like to know?"

"Anything. Anything at all that will help me to understand what sort of woman she is."

"She's a damn good woman. I've never known Jane to think of herself first."

"Was she ever married?"

"No. But there's plenty that asked her."

"Including you?"

He nodded his head and flipped the burned-down ciga-
te into the wind.

"I came close to asking her. I think she would have said
s."

"What kept you from asking her, Mr. Moon?"

"Man like me, why I'm not much of a catch. She de-
rved better than a man like me."

"You seem well-spoken and not a ruffian. Why would
u believe she would not think highly of you?"

"Don't judge everybody by how they speak or how they
ok, gal. I had my ways. They weren't all good."

"Yet you would help a dying woman find her daughter?"

"As I said, Jane's a friend. Friends count for something."

"I think she would have done well to marry you, Mr.
oon."

He watched as she went back inside the car and then he
ned his attention once more to the plains and the wind
at blew across them. It was a land that suffered only from
loneliness. It was a land that cradled its dead and toler-
d its living and kept a vigil over both. There was too
ich of it and yet, in some ways, not enough.

Black smoke billowed from the engine, and Hays lay up
ead.

Sassy was the first to spot them—Ben Moon and the
ung woman walking down the sidewalk. She had been
nding at the window of Jane's room, having just finished
lping Jane with her bath when she saw them.

"Lord, Miss Jane, but here comes that ol' Ben Moon and
has a young girl with him!"

Jane clasped a hand to her mouth. It was finally time for
r to meet her daughter, and she was uncertain.

"What will she think of me, Sassy? What will my Sa▮ think of me? Especially like this?"

"Don't be foolish, Miss Jane. She'll think you're j▮ what you are, her mammy."

"No. No she won't. She'll think I'm just a sick ▮ woman."

Sassy sat on the side of the bed and stroked her han▮

"You hesh such talk. You are a fine woman, graci▮ and kind. And that poor child will see how much you' been lovin' and missin' her the minute she lays eyes you."

"I'm afraid, Sassy. I'm afraid."

"I know you are."

They heard a knock. Sassy traded looks with Jane, th▮ opened the door.

"Jane, I've brought someone to see you," said Ben Mo▮

Sarah stepped into the room.

Ben Moon left them alone and walked down the str▮ to the nearest saloon.

"I'll have a whiskey, and do you know of anyone in to▮ that cuts stone?"

"You mean like a tombstone?" asked the bartender, sl▮ ing the glass of liquor toward the tall man.

He nodded.

"There is a fellow, an Italian name of Garbetti. Liv▮ east of town, about a mile out."

He rented a horse and wagon and rode out to Mr. G▮ betti's place. A number of marble stones were stacked ▮ the front yard.

The man who met him was a small, slight man with gr▮ black mustaches and coal black eyes and hair.

"Mr. Garbetti, I am told that you cut stones?"

"I do. I am the finest stonecutter in all of Kansas," s▮

e man with a broad smile. "I am the *only* stonecutter in
l of Kansas," he laughed. "At least the only *Italiano,* eh?"

"I'd like a stone cut."

"Sì. What do you want it to say?"

Ben Moon wrote out the name on a piece of paper and
nded it to the man. He read it.

"Is that all you want me to carve on it, this name?"

"Yes. It should be enough."

"Do you want to pick out a stone, then?"

"No. You do it. I'll trust you're judgment."

"When do you want it?"

"I'll wait, if you don't mind." When he saw the man's
uestioning look, he said, "I'd just as soon take it with me
 to have to come back."

"Sure, sure. It takes maybe an hour, maybe two, eh? How
ould you like some nice red wine while you wait? Rosa?"

plump woman with a cheerful face appeared in the door.

"Rosa, bring this gentleman some wine, eh? He's thirsty.
ist look at him."

He sat on an upside-down washtub in the yard and
atched the stonecutter work and sipped the red wine that
e man's wife had given him.

He listened to the ringing of the hammer on the cold
isel and watched as the chisel cut into the stone. Mr.
arbetti was very meticulous, very deliberate, examining
ch cut before continuing.

Finally, when the sun had crossed from east to west, the
ork was done.

"What do you think, eh?" asked the stonecutter.

"It'll do just fine, Mr. Garbetti. How much do I owe
ou?"

"Fifteen dollars. That's good Italian marble. It'll last a
ng time."

The stonecutter helped him load the marble on t
wagon; it weighed as much as an anvil.

They shook hands, and Ben Moon turned the rig towa
town.

He parked the wagon in front of the hotel and climb
the stairs to Jane's room. They were all three there—Jar
Sassy, and Sarah, their eyes wet from crying. He felt c
of place.

Jane's gaze rose to meet his. She started to speak. I
cut her off.

"I'm going to be gone for a couple of days," he sa
"There's some unfinished business I need to attend to."

Jane wiped tears from the corners of her eye and sa
"Are you coming back?"

He looked at her and said, "I'll be leaving first thing
the morning."

"Ben?"

"I'm glad it has all worked out, Jane." He looked ir
Sarah's expectant, uncertain eyes. "You two talk. Listen
one another."

He heard Jane call after him as he walked down the ha

At first light, he climbed aboard the wagon and "hawe
the horse and snapped the reins over its rump. Hays was
town still asleep and at its most peaceful.

He rode until the sun was straight up in the sky and th
took a rest before crossing a muddy brown stream that
did not know the name of. In the distance he could see
curl of gray smoke rising from the soddy.

Pearl was the first to spot the approaching wagon.

"Mama, somebody's coming."

Kid Joe and Fess Foley were atop the roof replacing s
that had been done in by the winter.

"Reckon who that'd be?" asked Fess Foley. Kid Joe's ey

re better than those of his daddy. He raised a hand to
ield out the glare of the sun.

After several minutes he declared, "It's Ben Moon come
ck!"

"Driving a wagon?" questioned the old man.

Pearl had come out of the house and stood in the yard.
e wind billowed her skirts.

"He's come back," she said. "Ben Moon has come back."
er mind raced with the reasons for his return. There was
ly one that she could think of, and it made her heart
tter.

They waited until Ben Moon pulled back on the reins
d brought the wagon to a halt.

Kid Joe said, "You are a surprise."

Pearl said, "You've returned to us."

Fess Foley said, "Climb down and we'll have a taste of
me sippin' whiskey and you can tell us why you're
re."

The two men drank a tin cup of the liquor, and everyone
ited for Ben Moon to tell them why he had come back.

"I hate to trouble you good folks more," he began, "but
eed to ask a final favor."

Pearl was hoping it would be to ask her parents for her
nd in marriage. She was already counting on the days
en she and Ben Moon would ride the frontier in reckless
shion—she, the bride of the Wild Desperado.

"You go right ahead and ask, Mr. Moon," said Fess Foley.

"I'd like to have Kid Joe lead me out to the place where
d's buried."

Pearl's bright and expectant face faded into disappoint-
ent.

"Sure," said Kid Joe's daddy. "But why?"

Ben Moon reached inside the wagon and removed burlap sack covering the gravestone.

"Ned and I weren't close, but we started out a job gether and he got killed trying to see it done. It's the le he's owed. A man ought to have something to show that was here."

Pearl, in spite of her disappointment at not having be asked to elope with him, thought Ben Moon gallant in thoughtfulness for a fallen companion.

"Sure, best to wait until morning to get a start; it' good half-a-day's ride. Supper will be on soon."

Kid Joe said, "Ma's cooking hog jowls, and her cornbr is something special."

"Fine," said Ben Moon. "That'll do just fine."

Pearl found herself walking away from the house in 1 disappointed state. She had so hoped that Ben Moon h come to rescue her from a life of drudgery, as she had 1 herself to believe life had become since Ben Moon's fi appearance.

She wandered down to a small stream that meandered the east of the sod house. A single willow tree not lar, around than her arm, nor taller than a man, leaned out o the cut bank of the tributary. It was, she thought, the o beauty within miles and miles.

Ben Moon, how could you not have come for me? S asked herself the bitter question over and over again.

At the whisper of boot steps against the budding gra she turned with a start.

"Pearl. Are you feeling all right?" It was Ben Moon, and handsome in a rough sort of way, the sort of way t any True Knight would appear. His startling gaze offe only concern as he stared into her eyes.

She bit down on her quivering lower lip to keep fr

ursting out in a bawl. Still, one or two tears managed to
ak from her eyes.

"I am . . . only . . . happy to . . . see you again," she
uttered.

"Well, I am glad to see you again as well," he said.

Her heart felt as if it were racing up into her throat.

"Pearl, I guess maybe I have been thoughtless in my
wn needs. I reckon now that I've had some time to re-
ect upon everything, there is something I would like to
ay to you."

Oh, dear!

"I'd be willing to bet hard money that you are the pret-
est girl in all of Kansas. And, if I were younger, I'd ask
our folks to let me come courting. They'd probably run
ie off, but I'd ask anyway." He took a step closer and lifted
er chin.

"Pearl, any man would be proud to have a good woman
ke you by his side. Someday, that'll happen. If it wouldn't
e too much to ask, I wonder if you might mind my stealing
ust one kiss from you. It'd sure be a memory that I'd be
ble to carry for a long time."

She thought she might not be able to speak at all, but
vhen she tried, she found that she could.

"You could steal all the kisses you wanted from me, Ben
Moon."

"I'd just like one," he said.

She closed her eyes and lifted her face.

It was a good kiss, she thought later that night while
ying in bed. It hadn't lasted long, nor had it made her ache
or more or made her burn with passion, whatever that was.
But, it was a good solid kiss that had made her happy and
iad made her realize that Ben Moon wasn't just treating

her like some foolish little girl. It was the kind of kiss th
a man would give to a woman, she decided.

She whispered his name and said, "I will always lo
you, Ben Moon, no matter where you are or where I an

Twenty-seven

Kid Joe was already waiting for him by the time he
raised up from the bed he had made himself under the
wagon. Pearl brought a platter of biscuits and churned
butter and fried ham. He walked stiffly to the water tank
and splashed the stinging cold water over his face and
neck.

Fess brought a pot of coffee and poured them each some
in tin cups. "Care for sugar?" he asked everyone.

Afterwards, Kid Joe harnessed the bay mare to the
wagon and said, "I'm ready to go when you are, Mr.
Moon."

Ben Moon turned to the others and said, "Thanks for
letting Kid Joe go with me." Then, they watched as Ben
Moon seated himself next to Kid Joe, who took the reins
and shouted "Haw! haw!" to the horse and snapped the
reins sharply over the mare's rump.

The wagon rattled along at a pace just slightly faster
than a man might walk and for a time neither Kid Joe
nor Ben Moon said anything. The prairie stretched out
before them, and all either of them could see was new
grass and sky.

"Pearl won't stop talking about you," said Kid Joe an
hour into the journey.

"She's a charming girl," said Ben Moon.

"I think she's in love with you. Ain't that silly of he▮

"Am I that old and run down?"

"Oh, no, Mr. Moon! I didn't mean it that way at all just mean that Pearl's awfully young to be thinking ab▮ being in love."

"Don't fool yourself, Kid. Women grow up knowing h▮ to love. It takes us men a long time to get the hang of ▮

"You've probably known a lot of women in your tir I'll bet," said Kid Joe.

"A few."

"Did you ever know any whores?"

"Some."

"I reckon soon enough, I'll be going into Hays to ▮ me a whore. I reckon I'm near old enough."

"I reckon maybe you are," said Ben Moon, giving K Joe the eye.

"I reckon another year, maybe, I'll be heading out on ▮ own altogether," said Kid Joe, warming to the conversatio

"Can't wait to see the elephant, huh, Kid?"

"Yes, sir!"

"Well, it's a world full of wonderment out there," sa Ben Moon, waving his arm before him.

"I bet you've seen it all, haven't you, Mr. Moon?"

"Just about, Kid. Just about."

"Well, I aim to see it, too, someday."

Kid Joe was a big strapping boy with an honest fac The sun had already begun to redden his neck and ears. ▮ possessed the eager eyes of a pup.

"It'd be hard to fault you, Kid, for wanting to see it a But it ain't all good what you're bound to see out there.

"I understand that, sir. I reckon that land is as full killers and lowlife as it is anything. But I figure I can ho my water without spilling it at the first sight of a badmar

d Joe offered up a broad smile and clucked the horse
o a trot.

They rode on across the sameness of land for several
re hours. Now and then Ben Moon took the reins while
d Joe took a harmonica out of his pocket and blew into

"I'm not the best." He grinned.

Ben Moon didn't mind.

They halted a few times so Ben Moon could stretch out
bad leg and walk around on it. And near noon, they
pped to eat a lunch of head cheese and crackers and cold
ffee. Ben Moon smoked a cigarette afterwards and
etched out on the grass and Kid Joe did the same and
y both took naps.

By mid-afternoon, Kid Joe turned the wagon off the trace
y had been following and down a slight slope.

"There it is," he said, pointing to the hump of disturbed
d several yards ahead.

They halted the wagon and unloaded the tombstone. Kid
e said, "I'll dig out a hollow so we can set her in."

Ben Moon studied the chiseled name NED BLUECORN
the marble slab while Kid Joe worked out a spot in the
ound to rest it in. It took several minutes, but soon enough
y had the gravestone in place, facing east.

"Indians have a thing about facing east in the mornings,"
id Ben Moon.

"I've heard that, too," said Kid Joe, "but I ain't sure why
y do."

"Indians are hard to figure out, Kid. Harder than
omen."

They finished their work, then stared down at the gray
one marker.

"I reckon when folks come by here," said Kid J[
"they'll at least know what his name was."

"Are you opposed to hard liquor, Kid?"

"No, sir. Although I ain't never had any."

"Well, it's time you did. There's no better an occasi[
for a man's first drink than a wedding or a funeral. Go a[
get the jug out of the wagon, and let's give ol' Ned a go[
send-off."

"Did *he* like the taste of hooch, Mr. Moon?"

"No, Kid, Ned was a teetotaller. For an Indian, tha[
something."

Kid Joe retrieved the jug from the wagon and handed[
to Ben Moon, who pulled the cork and raised it up to [
lips.

"Here's to Ned!" he declared and took a good swallo[

He handed the jug to Kid Joe, who took hold of it wi[
both hands.

"You don't have to if you don't want, Kid. Ol' Ned wou[
understand."

Without comment, Kid Joe took a swallow, coughed a[
sputtered, but held it all down.

"Ol' Ned would appreciate your grit, Kid."

Kid Joe looked at the late afternoon sky, a brassy s[
that would, in a matter of a couple more hours, lose its he[
and light.

"Do you want to make camp here for the night?" [
asked.

"No, Kid. Not here."

They turned toward the wagon. The rider was sitting [
stud horse not twenty yards away.

"Sorry I missed the party," said the rider, the sun to [
back so that his face was hidden in silhouette.

"Wasn't no party, mister," said Ben Moon, his sens[

easy at the sudden appearance of a man so far from the
in trace.

"He a friend of yours?" asked the man, indicating the
ave.

"Was," said Ben Moon.

"Handsome headstone," said the stranger. "A man de-
-ving of such concern must have been a special breed."

There was something old, familiar, about the man, the
ay he spoke, the way he sat a horse. Without knowing
to, Ben Moon knew that it was the Past sitting that horse.
mebody whose path he had once crossed. Friendly or no,
could not remember.

The angle of the sun notwithstanding, both Kid Joe and
en Moon could see the stranger was well armed; twin
volvers showed from his belt, and a Winchester rested
ross the pommel of his saddle.

Wind lifted the fringes of his buckskin jacket.

"Do we know each other?" asked Ben Moon.

"We did once," said the man, edging his horse slightly
oser.

"I don't recall," said Ben Moon.

"The way I hear it," said the man, "you've gone to seed.
guess when a man goes to seed, he can't be blamed for
t remembering."

Ben Moon was eliminating names in his mind, names of
unfighters he *could* recall, for this man was surely a gun-
ghter.

"Kid, move away," said Ben Moon.

"I've come to kill you, Moon," said the man.

"Did I do you some harm in the past, mister?"

"No."

"You were hired?"

"I was."

Ben gave Kid Joe the eye, and Kid Joe stepped away

"Easy, boy!" said the man. "Don't make any sude moves."

"Have you come to kill me or this boy here? He's or a homesteader."

"I can see what he is, Moon."

The man's horse danced its rump around, and the slant sunlight lit the man's features.

"Sam Pepper. I recall you now. You always were a snea sonofabitch." It was an angular face without expression not-easy-to-forget sort of face.

"Well, now, I can see you ain't gone to seed as much I've heard."

"I didn't know you to shoot innocent boys, Pepper."

"I'll shoot whatever they pay me to, Moon. Boys cluded."

"I reckon if that's the case," said Ben Moon, "times m be damn hard."

Kid Joe could see the man studying him, the cold ey looking into his own.

"Boy, if I were you, I'd head on out of here quick." K Joe looked at Ben Moon. Ben Moon nodded.

"Take off, Kid."

Kid Joe started for the wagon.

"Leave the wagon, boy! I'll be needing it to haul I carcass back to Hays."

"Why Hays?" asked Ben Moon.

"I need proof for the widow that I killed you. Newspar account or some such. She's demanding in that way."

Kid Joe felt the press of the Starr under his coat; he h stuck it in his belt that morning. He had moved off to t side, thirty feet maybe. It would have to be done all at on

couldn't miss if he were to try it. If he missed, the man
the stud horse would kill them both.

He felt sweat creep down his sides and the back of his
ck. He'd practiced a lot with the Starr ever since Ben
oon had given it to him. But shooting bean cans off a
imp with plenty of time to take aim and fire sure hadn't
ade him sweat as he was sweating right now.

He was walking away from the man, walking away as if
were leaving. To do it, he'd have to reach inside his coat,
ll the piece, cock it, turn, aim, and fire—just that quick.
amned if he knew if he had the nerve to do it!

"Well, I hope the widow paid you well," he heard Ben
oon saying.

"Well enough," said Sam Pepper. "I believe there might
en be a bonus in it. In spite of her dry ways, I find myself
tracted to her. Do you want it in the front or the back?
r does it matter to you?"

Sam Pepper heard the mechanism of a pistol being cocked.
e turned partway around in the saddle, yanking one of the
volvers from his belt as he did so.

Kid Joe had managed not to drop the pistol in the pulling.
e had done it smoothly and more swiftly than he had
nagined he could. He saw the man turn in the saddle, saw
m raise a long-barreled revolver, and aim it.

The double blasts of the pistols crashed the air. Kid Joe
lt the punch of the bullet hit him high, up near his neck.
felt as if someone had busted him with an ax handle, and
knocked him flat on his back.

Sam Pepper cried, "Sonofabitch!" and pitched from his
ddle.

Ben Moon grabbed the revolver from his hand and the
her from his belt and stepped back quickly. Blood was

staining the buckskin jacket and leaking out between S
Pepper's fingers.

"That goddamn kid shot me!"

"He shot you damn good, Pepper."

"Did I kill him?"

Ben Moon walked over to where Kid Joe was half-s
ting up holding a bloody spot between his neck and sho
der.

"Kid, does it feel like you're dying?" Ben Moon ask
taking away Kid Joe's hand so he could look at the jagg
bloody hole.

"It hurts durn bad, Mr. Moon. I can't lift up my arm

"Went clean through and out the other side, Kid. Bust
your collar bone, I'd say."

"Well, do you reckon I will die?"

"Not today, Kid." Ben Moon reached in his pocket a
took out a silk kerchief and stuffed it in Kid Joe's wou

"What about him?" asked Kid Joe.

"You killed him, Kid. He's not dead yet, but you kill
him sure as anything. Lie back easy now, son. Let me
and finish this business."

"Mr. Moon?"

"What is it, Kid?"

"You're not going to put another bullet in him?"

"Well, Kid, that'd be sort of the humane thing to c
seeing as how he's shot in the worst place a man can g
shot in."

"No, Mr. Moon. Please don't do it!!"

"Well, what do you want us to do, Kid? Sit around a
wait for him to die on his own accord?"

"Yes, sir. It wouldn't be the Christian thing to do, sho
ing him down while he's already wounded so."

"I'm not a Christian, Kid."

"I'll ask you not to do it for me then. Ain't I the one
at saved your life?"

"Yeah, Kid. You did."

"Then you owe it to me not to kill him. Not like this."

"Okay, Kid, you win. We'll let ol' Sam Pepper die on his
vn accord, but he ain't going to like it much."

Ben Moon walked back to where Sam Pepper lay on his
ck, his gaze fixed on the glaring sky overhead.

"Finish me off, Moon. This hurts like hell."

"I can't, Pepper."

"Why not?"

"Kid made me promise not to. He said it wouldn't be
e Christian thing to do. I tried to argue with him, but you
ow how stubborn homesteaders can be."

"To hell with him!"

"Would you like a taste of whiskey? I have some in that
g yonder."

"I should've shot that ugly kid first thing," said Sam
pper. "I don't know why I didn't."

"Do you want the whiskey or not?"

"Hell yes!"

He held the jug to Sam Pepper's mouth while the
ounded man swallowed. The whiskey had the effect of a
se of whooping cough, and it took a full minute for the
asms to quit.

"Christ!" said Sam Pepper. "I believe I am dying!" Then,
ithout bothering to close either eye, he did.

"Come on, Kid," said Ben Moon, lifting Kid Joe up
d into the bed of the wagon. "Let's get you home. Your
a sure ain't going to be very damn happy with me over
is."

"Aren't you going to bury him, Mr. Moon?"

"Jesus, Kid. You want me to say a prayer over him, too?"

"It would be kind on your part."

Ben Moon looked into the honest, open face of Kid J
and could not avoid those imploring calf eyes the Kid w
giving him.

"Next time you shoot a man, Kid, do it when I ai
around."

Twenty-eight

Pearl wept and so did her mother when they saw Kid Joe ~~l~~ing in the back of the wagon. Then, like the frontier ~~w~~omen they were, they carried him inside the soddy, set ~~w~~ater to boiling, peeled off his bloody clothes, and cared ~~fo~~r him.

Ben Moon told Fess Foley the story as the two men sat ~~in~~ the front yard.

"Sam Pepper," said Fess Foley. "Damn if I can believe ~~th~~at the dangerous Sam Pepper has shot my boy—or that ~~m~~y boy has shot him."

"There seemed no choice in the matter," said Ben Moon. ~~"~~Kid Joe proved himself worthy when the chips were ~~d~~own."

Inside the house, Pearl said: "Kid, you are a hero, for ~~yo~~u have laid low that notorious badman, Sam Pepper. Ev~~er~~yone will be talking about it when they hear the news."

"Hush," said Pearl's ma. "I won't listen to murderous ~~ta~~lk in my house. It is bad enough that violence has come ~~to~~ visit this household without any one of us speaking of ~~it~~ as if it were some sort of glory."

Kid Joe said, "I feel sorry for Sam Pepper, even though ~~h~~e did try to kill me."

Outside the house, Fess Foley said, "I hope this hasn't ~~af~~fected my boy too badly, shooting another man."

Fess Foley's words hung in the air like the smoke fro Ben Moon's cigarette.

It was a long time before Kid Joe's daddy spoke aga When he did, his words came out slow, achingly, as if th were being pulled up from the center of his soul.

"I know it wasn't your fault that Kid Joe took a bull Mr. Moon. But nonetheless, I reckon I have to ask you leave first thing in the morning and not come back. Ev since Kid and I first found you, his head has been fill with cotton and thoughts of being a pistoleer. Your givi him your old Starr didn't help any. I reckon now he h seen the light. At least I hope he has."

"I am sorry it had to come to this," said Ben Moon.

"So am I."

"I'll be gone before sunup."

"I'll have Martha make you up some sandwiches to ta along on your journey."

"It's not necessary."

"I'll have her do it anyway."

They shook hands, and Ben Moon prepared his bedro Fess Foley went inside the soddy and soon turned out the lights.

The prairie lay as still as it ever had. Ben thought of Ja and Sarah and Kid Joe and Pearl. He thought of Ned Blu corn and Fess Foley and the way Sam Pepper had look at the moment just before he died with his eyes wide ope

He stared up at the sky full of stars and heard the wi whisper along the grass and never knew the prairie to more lonely. Or was it just him?

He thought about all the men he had hunted and the on that had hunted him. He thought about dead boys and w ows and mean horses and bad whiskey and forgotten nigh

You ain't come to much, Ben Moon. You sure ain't.

Sleep came hard.

Fess Foley came out of the soddy; pulling up his braces. thin thread of light appeared on the eastern horizon. Ben Moon was already dressed.

"I'd like to borrow a saddle," said Ben Moon.

"Are you up to riding a horse?" asked Kid Joe's daddy.

"I have some business to take care of; a saddle horse ould see it done sooner."

Fess Foley went to the corral, lifted down a Texas double g, and set it on the back of the bay mare.

"When I get done with my business," said Ben Moon, ghtening down the cinches, "I'll have it shipped back to u."

Fess Foley nodded.

"Is Kid Joe awake?"

"He might be."

"I'd like a word with him."

Fess Foley stepped aside.

Ben Moon entered the soddy. Pearl and Martha were orking over the great cast-iron stove; he could feel the at coming off it.

"He's in there," said Pearl, nodding to the space beyond e suspended blanket.

"Kid? Are you awake?"

Kid Joe's eyelids fluttered open. He looked as pale as his nen.

"Mr. Moon."

"Kid, I just wanted to say thanks for saving my life."

Kid Joe's gaze drifted to the sod wall beside his bed.

"I hadn't meant to kill that man, Mr. Moon."

"I know, Kid."

"Pearl says I'm some sort of hero for shooting the infaous Sam Pepper." Tears leaked from the boy's eyes.

"You don't have to talk about it, Kid."

"She don't understand, Pearl don't. It ain't like that. ain't like the dime novels tell it."

"No, Kid, it ain't."

"Do you know if Mr. Pepper had a family?"

"I can't say, Kid."

"Mr. Moon?"

"Yeah, Kid?"

"I guess I won't be needing your Starr."

"I guess not."

"You take care of yourself, Mr. Moon."

"Same with you, Kid. I'll be seeing you."

He walked past the two women and out into the ya Fess Foley held the reins to the mare.

They shook hands but did not speak further. Fess Fo took a deep breath and let it out as he watched Ben Mo touch his heels to the mare and start her into a trot. Pe and Martha came out and stood in the stone light next Kid Joe's daddy.

"I knew that trouble was ours to be had the first tim laid eyes on that poor man," said Fess Foley's wife. "I do mean to sound uncaring, but if it were ours to do all ov again, I would not allow him to come here."

Fess Foley remained silent. Pearl squeezed the tears fr her eyes and said, "He is a wandering knight without hea or kin. I feel full of sorrow for him."

"I wouldn't feel too sorry for him, child," said Fess Fol "I'd save my sorrow for those who oppose him."

"Amen for that," said Pearl's mother.

Billy Tibbs and three of his deputies—Joe Stolley, R Jerrod, and Silas Odell—gathered up their shotguns and l them in the crooks of their arms. It was time for evening rounds.

He had supper on his mind. It had been a long slow day, and he was thinking about supper.

Billy Tibbs pulled the brass watch from his vest pocket, snapped open the face, and studied the black spider-hands of the Elgin.

It was nearly six in the evening.

Their boots clomped on the boardwalk as they moved along—two in front, two in back. They took turns testing the doorknobs of the closed businesses along Front Street, the section that the locals had taken to calling "The Plaza."

They moved past the Lady Gay Saloon, and Ed Skinner's Chop House. It was too early for the revelry to have begun. Most folks were at home having their supper. Billy Tibbs wished he were having his supper.

Thirty dollars a month didn't seem worth it to maybe get his head shot off by some damn rowdy Texas cowboy. But, the position of Town Marshal afforded an enterprising fellow other opportunities such as partnerships in the steady business of gambling and prostitution.

Pork Chops. Billy Tibbs had his mind set on pork chops for supper. Pork chops and fried potatoes and cole slaw and a good glass of cold beer.

They strolled past the Long Branch Saloon. It was fairly quiet. Deputy Stolly dropped out of the group, saying he wanted a beer and would catch up in a few minutes.

Billy and the other two men reached the end of Front Street, crossed over, and started back the other side. They passed LeMore's Pharmacy and the lumberyard.

Red Jerrod said he had to make water and stepped into an alley. Billy Tibbs and Silas Odell continued on.

They had neared the harness shop when a man stepped

from the shadows. There was something suspicious about
the man.

"Whoa there, mister, can't you see we're armed?" shouted
Silas Odell.

The man said nothing.

"Step into the light so's we can get a look at you," ordered Billy Tibbs, swinging the shotgun off his arm and
taking hold of it with both hands.

Silas Odell took a step backwards and caught his heel
on the edge of the walk and fell over backwards.

"I said move, goddamn it," said Billy raising up the shotgun.

The man stepped out of the shadows and into the light
of a nearby restaurant, where several people stopped eating
their food and looked at the men outside.

As soon as Billy Tibbs saw the face of the man, he said:
"Jesus H. Christ! Junebug Little, what are you doing coming out of the shadows on armed men?"

Junebug Little had the confused look of a drunkard. He
raised the palms of both hands.

"I didn't know who it was," he said.

"I ought to lock you up."

"Did I scare you?"

"It ain't time to be funny, Junebug. Get the hell out of
here before I fill your ass with both barrels." Silas Odell
regained his feet and brushed off the seat of his pants, and
he and Billy watched Junebug Little stumble his way down
the street.

"Crazy old bastard!" said Billy Tibbs.

They finished their rounds and each headed in different
directions.

"I'll see you boys tomorrow," said Billy Tibbs, feeling

the hunger gnawing at his guts. He waited until the others left, then took the keys and locked the office.

He took his supper at Ed Skinner's Chop House and was disappointed that there were no pork chops left. He had had his mind set on pork chops. He ate without cheer, and Ed Skinner personally apologized for the oversight.

"Next time I come in here," said Billy, "I expect to get pork chops and plenty of them."

"I'll see to it," said Ed Skinner.

"Well, maybe Blonde Marie won't be so disappointing," said Billy. "I think I'll just pay her a visit. This food has made my stomach sour."

Billy Tibbs made his way down the street to the Lady Gay Saloon and found Blonde Marie sitting at a table with a man he knew to be a bachelor by the name of Stiggs.

"Git lost!" he told Stiggs. "Marie's with me tonight."

Blonde Marie was a large fleshy woman with short, curly blond hair and ruby cheeks.

"I was working on something," she said crossly to Billy.

"Him?" said Billy.

"At least *he's* willing to pay."

"Let's grab a bottle and go back to your crib," said Billy. "My nerves are shot, and my gut is feeling aggravated."

She knew not to argue with him; he'd just get rough with her. "Sure, Billy," she agreed. "Anything you say."

Blonde Marie's crib lay to the rear of the Lady Gay. She and Billy stepped out the back door, across a narrow alley-way, and inside the small structure. Blonde Marie struck a match to a kerosene lantern. The yellow light revealed a bunk, a small dresser, a chair, and a chamber pot.

"Well, let's get to it, gal," said Billy Tibbs. "I've got an urge that needs tending."

It didn't take long, Billy's urge to be tended to. Afterwards, he lay wrapped up in the blankets, drinking from the bottle of rye.

Marie said, "Couldn't you pay me just this once, Billy?"

"I don't pay, Marie. You ought to know that by now."

"Why," she said, "just because you're the law?"

"That's right, woman! Just because I am the law."

The door kicked open, and Ben Moon stepped inside the room.

"What the hell . . ."

"Pay the woman, Billy. Just this once."

"Moon!"

"Well, at least you didn't forget."

Blonde Marie bunched herself in a corner.

"You must be cold without your clothes on," said Ben Moon. "Go ahead and get dressed and take what he owes you out of his britches."

"Damn you, Moon! What gives you the right to come busting in on me?"

"You should've let it rest when you had the chance, Billy. You crossed over the line when you decided to become an assassin; you ain't cut out for the work. Assassins are good at what they do."

"I don't know what the hell you're talking about, Moon."

"Yes, you do," said Ben Moon, reaching for the shotgun that Billy had propped up in one corner of the room.

"I see you still carry this old Hamilton around with you, Billy. What do you have it loaded with now? Double-ough buckshot?"

"Dimes!" spat Billy. "Goddamn dimes in case I run into lowlife like you, Ben Moon!" Billy's hand snaked under the pillow and came out holding a Colt pocket pistol.

The twin blasts of the shotgun shattered the air and left it filled with blue, acrid smoke.

"How's it feel, Billy?" asked Ben Moon, lowering the
cattergun. "How's it feel to be murdered in your own blan-
ets?"

Blonde Marie tried her best to keep from biting off her
wn tongue as she stared at the riddled corpse of Billy
ibbs. With great effort, she turned her gaze to the man
anding just inside the room. She saw the clear, colorless
yes move from the destruction upon the bed to her.

"Forget what you've seen here," he said.

She started to speak. Her tongue clucked inside her
outh, making noises as if she was trying to speak. He
rned and left her there like that, trying to speak.

Twenty-nine

He reached Hays on the day of Jane's funeral. She'd die
on Tuesday.

"I bought her a beautiful dress," said Sarah. "A whit
one with lots of lace."

"And a rosewood casket that we had to send all the wa
to Kansas City for," said Sassy. "She looks so peaceful an
lovely in that dress and rosewood casket. I know she woul
like everything we did for her."

A black hearse with glass panels pulled by matching gra
horses with black-and-silver bridles carried the rosewoo
casket from Tolivar & Bros. Funeral Parlor over to the Firs
Baptist Church, whose whiteness shone more brightly tha
any other building in Hays and whose belfry bell clange
solemnly from the tower.

"I believe everyone on the prairie will hear the bells toll
ing for Miss Jane," said Sassy.

The gathered sang "Tender Thy Mercy" and "God's Glc
rious Grace" and "A Walk Down Heaven's Road."

Pastor Pogue, a stick of a man in a black suit and dingy
yellow paper collar, leaned himself across the top of hi
lectern and spoke in a stentorian voice that belied his bird
like constitution.

Pastor Pogue's sermon had to do with sin and fallin
from grace and redemption and forgiveness and love an

eavenly rewards. But the few that had gathered in the hard
ews of the church fell inattentive after the first twenty
ninutes of the sermon for it all seemed to run together,
hose things about love and forgiveness and sin and redemp-
ion.

Ben Moon stood outside the open doors and smoked a
igarette and only half-listened to the droning voice within.

"Why don't you come in and sit with us?" Sarah had
sked when they'd first arrived.

He had declined, ashamed of his appearance. He had had
o time for a change of clothes or a bath or even a shave.

It seemed damned awful that Jane was gone. It seemed
ven worse to him that he hadn't been there at the last.

Finally, Pastor Pogue gave it up and said, "Amen."

Ben helped carry the casket to the hearse, then mounted
he bay mare and followed the small procession out to the
ast of town and up a slight rise to where a fancy wrought-
ron fence enclosed a cemetery.

Two men in coveralls stood holding onto spades near an
pen grave. They put out their cigarettes and wandered away
vhen the hearse pulled up to the gate.

Sarah and Sassy wept openly as the rosewood coffin was
owered into the grave on ropes. Pastor Pogue had saved a
ew words for the last, but not many.

Finally, only the three of them remained: Sarah, Sassy,
nd Ben Moon.

"I only wish I could have had a chance to know her
etter," said Sarah.

"Miss Jane was a fine woman," said Sassy. "She treated
ne as if I were her own. I don't know what I will do with
nyself now that she is gone."

"You will come and stay with me," said Sarah.

"I don't believe I could live here in such flat country,"

said Sassy. "No offense. The wind seems to never leave
body alone. It sort of causes me to grit my teeth afte
awhile."

"We won't be living here, Sassy," said Sarah.

"Where then?"

"Montana Territory. My mother left me the deed to th
Big House. I intend to go back there. The way she spok
of it, I feel I must go and see for myself the happy plac
she left."

"It's a whorehouse," said Ben Moon. "Didn't she tell yo
that?"

Sassy said, "Oh, Lord!"

Sarah shifted her gaze from Sassy to Ben Moon.

"If you are trying to shock me or dissuade me, M
Moon, you have failed. My mother told me everythin
about herself and her life and her business. She kept n
secrets from me. The way I see it, I have to become inde
pendent, as she had to. I have to make my way throug
life, just like her. And even though she left me a small sun
it will not be enough to last me forever. I see nothing wron
with operating my mother's business."

"There are other ways to make a living."

"For men, maybe. But for a woman, out here on th
frontier, pray tell me what, Mr. Moon?"

"Schoolteacher."

"Not interested."

"Seamstress."

"I might as well go straight to the poorhouse and as
them to take me in."

"You could get married."

"I will someday, but when I'm ready, not for the purpos
of relying on a man to care for me."

She had Jane's spit and fire, and the greenness of her eyes turned emerald with defiance.

"I look at it purely as a business decision, Mr. Moon, not as a moral one. What honor is there in being impoverished or enslaved to those who would keep their foot on your neck? My mother realized that more than anyone. She survived, Mr. Moon, and I intend to as well."

She turned her attention back to Sassy.

"We will be partners," she said. "We will split the profits and share the work of running a proper place. Are you willing?"

"Yes, ma'am, I am."

"Then let's get started."

Ben Moon waited until they had gone. Then, stiffly, he kneeled on one knee and removed his pinch-crowned Stetson and held it in both hands.

"Jane, I'm sorry I wasn't here for you at the end. Not that it would have made a difference on your part, although I'd like to believe it would have. It would have meant something to me." He paused, swallowed, touched the fresh-turned soil.

"She's a fine girl, Jane, Sarah is. A little strong-headed maybe. Like you were. I'm glad you got the time with her. I guess I'm more glad she got the time with you." The wind danced across the little cemetery and blew at his hair and buffeted his clothes.

"It's not going to be the same without you around, woman. I can tell you that. We should've gotten married, Jane, you and I. We should've gotten married and raised that little girl ourselves and been a family. What the hell happens to people like us?"

He felt himself choking back the emotion.

"Jane, I hate like hell to leave you here alone. I know

how much you loved Montana. Damned if you didn't love
Montana. Well, I guess there's not much left for me to say
Except, I love you, Jane. I always did."

He set the hat back on his head in a deliberate fashion,
curling the brim with the palms of his hands, and giving it
a final tug. He mounted the bay mare, allowed himself one
final glance at the open grave, then reined the horse's head
around and rode down the slope.

He caught up with the carriage that Sarah and Sassy were
riding in.

"I've decided to go back to Montana with you," he said
slowing the mare to a walk alongside the carriage.

Oh, Lordy, thought Sassy with dread.

"Well, it is a free country, Mr. Moon," said Sarah. "I
reckon you can go wherever you want."

"Well, where I want is Montana," said Ben Moon. "I
figure you'll need yourself a man there at that new business
of yours to keep some order."

"To maintain proper behavior among the gentlemen that
will come calling."

"Exactly."

"Do you have any experience in such matters, Mr. Moon
maintaining order?"

"Some."

"How much would you require for your services, Mr
Moon?"

"Room and board and three blankets in the winter."

"Seems fair. I suppose a man would be good to have
around, wouldn't you agree, Sassy?"

"If anybody would be good at scaring off trouble, i
would be *him,* Miss Sarah."

"Yes, I reckon maybe he would be," Sarah said with a
smile.

"Just one question," he said.

"Yes, Mr. Moon."

"Did Jane tell you everything while you were with her?"
She searched his clear eyes with her own.

"Yes, everything."

"Then you know."

"Yes, Mr. Moon. I know who you are."

"Do you still want me to go with you to Montana?"

"Yes, Mr. Moon. I want nothing more than for you to
go with us back to Montana. It is your home now as well
as ours."

For the first time she could recall, Sassy saw that ol' Ben
Moon smile as he kicked his horse into a trot as if he'd
just been told he was something special.

Lordy!

THE SURVIVALIST SERIES
by Jerry Ahern